LEVON'S PREY

A VIGILANTE JUSTICE THRILLER BOOK 10

CHUCK DIXON

ROUGH
EDGES
PRESS

ROUGH
EDGES
PRESS

Published in the United States by Wolfpack Publishing, Las Vegas

Rough Edges Press
An Imprint of Wolfpack Publishing
5130 S. Fort Apache Rd. 215-380
Las Vegas, NV 89148
roughedgespress.com

Paperback ISBN 978-1-68549-121-5
eBook ISBN 978-1-68549-120-8
LCCN 2022938476

LEVON'S PREY

1

It was only a practice game, but the boys were hustling hard.

Shirts versus skins. The shirts were green singlets trimmed in gold, Mt. Clara H.S. embroidered on the chests and backs. Both teams shiny with sweat. The squeak of sneakers on the high polished wood echoed off the walls of the near empty gym. The coach ran along the sides, offering encouragement and cautions to both sides.

"Good coverage, Jay. That's a foul, Nick. Watch your sides, Kenny." The coach's voice was husky, winded from trying to keep up.

"Which one's yours?"

Bruce Kingsley turned from his seat on the bleachers to look at the man seated on the row behind him. He was a stranger to Bruce. There was only a half dozen other parents here watching the practice. This man wasn't a regular. He'd remember a man like this if he'd met him before. Broad in the shoulders under a black leather coat over a dark shirt. The clothes set off the whiteness of the man, easily the whitest white man Bruce had ever seen. Not an albino but damned near. Close-cropped blond hair turning silver above the ears. Eyes the color of a swimming pool set in lashes so pale as to be invisible.

"That one," Bruce said, pointing at his son Jamal, now leaping above the boys crowded beneath the net for a textbook lay-up.

"Your boy's got game," the pale man said.

"He's not actually my boy. My wife had two kids when we married. They were little then."

"And you're being the good stepdad."

Bruce sensed disinterest in the man's lazy reply. Maybe it was just the heavy Bama drawl in the man's voice.

"I'm trying to be."

"The boy has plans when he graduates." It was a statement rather than a question.

"He's looking at schools."

"Bet some are lookin' at *him*." A mocking tone now, a note of superiority. Was this guy psyching him?

"One of these kids yours?" Bruce asked, shifted in his seat to regard the man. He turned back to the court when some of the parents began applauding. Jamal was getting back slaps from both sides of the game. Bruce missed the play talking to this yokel.

"Naw. Naw," the man said. "I'm here on business."

"With the school?"

"With you, Bruce."

Bruce swung back to the man. The man was leaning forward on his bench, elbows on knees, large heavy hands dangling. There were gnarled ridges across the knuckles of both hands. Their faces closer now, Bruce could see lumps of scar tissue on the man's brows. When the man smiled, as he did now, he revealed too-perfect, too-white teeth between lips that showed signs of being split in several places sometime in the past.

"You and me have business? Now?"

Bruce was getting annoyed now at this man's amused attitude. He'd met good old boys like this before. Always slow to get to the point. In love with their own corn pone charm. Bruce considered himself to be blind to race, giving every man or woman a chance to prove themselves. Taking people as they came. But he had to admit, a certain brand of white folks gave him a pain.

"You put in a bid for a contract to lay floors and foundation in Monroe County."

"You talkin' about the parking garage at the courthouse annex?"

"That's the one. Sweet contract. That's how many tons of pour? Sixty yards times three? Close to fifty thousand tons of 'crete."

"Closer to seventy, seventy-five, with the ramps and footing," Bruce corrected.

"Big job. That's a lotta truckloads."

"Job that big? We'll mix on site."

"Job that big," the pale man said, his smile opening to show more of his phony teeth.

"What's your interest here? I'm here to watch my boy play." Bruce turned back to watch the teams charge down the court, trying to make sense of the play.

"My interest is *your* interest, Bruce. This ain't so much a business offer as a word of advice."

Bruce turned back. The pale man touched fingers

to his shoulder, leaning closer behind him. A pinky ring with a pale lavender stone was out of place on the calloused sausage fingers.

"You need to withdraw that bid. You need to tell them you overextended yourself or like that. Your reach exceeded your grasp, you follow that?"

"Why would I do that?" Bruce shrugged to remove the man's fingers from his jacket.

"So maybe your boy there gets offered a scholarship to state. A full boat to be a Hornet. Grease on the skids to go pro. Talented as that boy is."

"We can get along without your help." Bruce turned back to the game, blind to what was going on.

"Or maybe. Just maybe." The man leaned closer, his breath on Bruce's ear, stretching the words out like he had all day and nowhere to be. "Your boy breaks a leg. Or two even. Real bad breaks. The kind that takes months for rehab and still he'll never walk right again. And running? Shit. He won't *never* run again."

Bruce's mouth and throat went dry. He'd been threatened before. Anyone in the contracting business had heard their share of dire promises over territories, unions and favoritism. He wouldn't be where he was now, the second largest paving business in the county and the largest minority-owned concrete business in the state, if he backed down to every redneck motherfucker who came around.

Only there was something in this man's voice that made him a believer. The fact that he'd never seen this particular man before lent weight to that. This guy was something new, something more dangerous.

His eyes found Jamal on the court and watched him, legs flexing, muscles bunching, leaving the ground to soar up above the pack and slam the ball down dead center through the hoop. The boy dropped to the floor, the pride clear in his eyes. A skin caught the rebound of a shirt's fingers. The other boys hooted and clapped as they broke up under the board to chase after the ball. Jamal spared a look to the stands, seeking Bruce out. When he found him, he offered his stepdad a beaming smile and a nod before joining the play downcourt.

When Bruce turned back to respond to the pale man the bench behind him was empty.

2

The face grinned at him, eyes wide, lots of teeth showing against green skin, through the scope lens.

"I don't think I ever shot anyone who looked this happy," Levon said, as he sighted down the range. The modified SIG Sauer propped on a sandbag rest.

"I always tried to never look at their faces," Wesley said, crouched to squint through the spotter scope set up next to Levon.

"But you still remember them." It wasn't a question. Levon made a fine adjustment to the dial atop the scope.

"Yeah. Put that shit aside then. Deal with it later. Still dealing."

"You give them faces even when you didn't see them. That's your memory filling in the blanks."

Two hundred yards away, the .308 punched a hole in the center of the grinning watermelon. Chunks of pink meat and white rind sprayed from the exit wound.

The sharp crack of the rifle came back to them as a staccato echo from the trees that lined either side of the holler called Sugar Run. This was once the rifle and shotgun range for the local Klan klavan. The range and nearby compound had been abandoned after Levon chased off the last two members, one of them a cousin of his. Now it was the home, for now at least, of Wesley Ruskin, a former Army Ranger Levon had found living rough up a holler even more remote than this one.

Together they mowed the cogon grass flat and bush-hogged the brush away to extend the range to its current two hundred plus yard depth. Only Wesley never did any shooting when Levon visited to use the range. Levon never pressed him, not about anything.

"Head shot. Clean kill. That's one dead piece of fruit," Wesley said and stood up from the range table built of 2x4s with a plywood top.

"You want to give it a go?" Levon held the rifle out after flipping the safety in place.

"And waste another fine watermelon? Not this brother." Wesley smiled, waving a hand before him.

"You know, if I made that joke. . ."

"You'd be a racist. *Fuck* that, bro. You *are* a racist. A born and bred in your bones racist. How could you *not* be?" But Wesley was laughing, a throaty chuckle that brought out a rare grin on Levon's face.

"Fuck you," Levon said.

"See? *See* that? You're a nigger-hating son of a bitch just like I said."

"Hand me the M4," Levon said. "Let's put this happy asshole out his misery."

Wesley held out the modified rifle. A heavier model, chrome-lined barrel and reinforced receiver and action. He turned his eye to the spotter scope and listened as Levon charged the weapon. He could see the other man take a slow intake of breath then the extended hiss as Levon let it out while laying the reticles on the distant target. Less of a crack than a boom. Wesley watched through the scope as the melon flew to bits in a wet spray.

"What the hell was that?" he turned to Levon removing the magazine and ejecting the live round that had fed into the chamber.

"Beowulf round."

"You planning on doing some more hunting?" They both knew the brand of hunting Wesley referred to.

"Nope. Just don't think I should lose my edge. Besides, I always liked shooting and I have lots of older rounds to go through."

They each took up a rifle to carry back to the doublewide that lay at the far end of open ground framed all around by tree-covered hills.

"So, that's all over for you?"

"Yeah. I'm in the moonshine business now. My uncle's serious about getting that up on its feet. You know, there's a job waiting if you ever want one."

"Not sure that's the line of work I'd want to get into."

"Saw a sign out in front of the Burger King over in Haley. They're looking for people."

"I cleaned all the grease pits I'm ever gonna," Wesley said.

"Not your line. I get it."

"Look," Wesley said when they'd reached Levon's Avalanche and set the rifles down on the open tailgate, "I don't like taking from you like this, bro. And I know you told me you have more than enough.

But I will repay you someday. I mean that."

"No need to even mention it." Levon slid the rifles into padded bags, the magazines going into pouches on the sides. He'd clean them at home in his shop.

"You want a coffee? I can at least offer you that."

"Sure. Can't stay long. I told my uncle I'd help out today."

They sat at the long table inside the doublewide and Wesley poured them both mugs of strong coffee. The inside of the prefab had changed from its role as a meeting house for the KKK into more of a man cave in the months since Wesley had moved in. He'd cleaned up a ratty old sofa and used a staplegun to reupholster the frame with canvas sail cloth. With Levon's help he'd closed off part of the large open room with a couple of partition walls to help contain the heat from the wood stove during the cold months. Wesley had taped and spackled and painted and now the room looked more like part of a house than it had before.

The rebel battle flag left behind by the klavan hung on one of the new walls. The bookcase that used to be full of Klan literature was now stacked with some former grand wizard's vintage *Playboy* collection Wesley'd found among the effects left behind. There were also some paperbacks Levon had picked up for him. Wesley liked science fiction and was a closet Trekkie.

There was a stack of newspapers on a chair by the table. Some lay open to their crossword puzzle pages, the squares partly filled in.

"You sure you're out of the hunting business?" Wesley said as he poured creamer into his mug.

"I made a promise to myself and to my girls."

"You think you made a difference?"

"I think I stopped some bad things from happening to people who didn't deserve it."

"And made some bad things happen to people who did."

Levon stirred his coffee even though he took it black and eyed the pile of old papers.

"You know, it's okay to throw away the papers I bring you."

"I'm working through the crosswords. And sometimes I don't get to the articles right away."

"Okay. I gotta go," Levon said after draining his mug. "When you're caught up on your puzzles you think about that job. Pay's good and my uncle'd love to have someone to yell at other than me."

"I'll keep it in mind, bro." Wesley watched Levon step out into the morning light and heard the Avalanche's tires crunch away across the gravel.

He turned his eyes to a folded section of the *Huntsville Times* and pulled it toward him. He flipped the pages of a three-month-old newspaper until he came to an item on page eight, a single column story.

BREAKING NEWS
LOCAL GAS EXPLOSION LEAVES
14 DEAD IN GEORGIA HOUSE

A ruptured gas line is being blamed for an explosion and resulting fire that left fourteen dead at what was supposed to be a New Year's Eve party outside Brillings, GA last night. The home, belonging to Edward and Patricia Dutton, was "a total loss," according to one firefighter at the scene. State police, state inspectors and officials from Georgia Natural Gas held a press conference in Albany to assure the public that the gas lines are safe and that this was an unusual occurrence brought on by homeowner negligence.

3

Special agent Larry Crozier wasn't feeling particularly special this morning.

Even given his one-on-one closed-door meeting with an assistant deputy director.

This was a debrief, an audit, a goddamned workout, the end of the kind of thankless shit job he'd come to expect in his twentieth year with the Bureau.

"Give me the high points," the ADD said from behind his immaculate desk. He was dipping a bag of herbal tea into a steaming mug.

"May I?" Larry asked, gesturing with the manila folder he lifted from his lap.

The ADD nodded and pursed his lips to blow on his tea.

Larry opened the file atop the desk. It was thick with reports and forms. All the required FBI documents stapled together with the ballistic and forensic findings from Georgia CID. The folder was especially weighty because the case came with a strict order that nothing be stored or transmitted electronically. It was paper all the way on this one. Orders come down from the AG, apparently.

"I have a summary," Larry said, lifting two pages of a double-spaced document.

"Give me the high points of *that* then. Tell me what's most pertinent." The ADD offered a simpering smile that turned to a wince when he diverted his glance to the phone on his desk. More pressing business awaited.

"Long story short, sir, we have nothing new after three months of investigation." Larry was relieved he'd not be asked to read the summary word for word. "We don't know much more than we knew on the seventh of January."

"No suspects?"

"It appears to be a single shooter using multiple weapons. None of these weapons were left at the scene. Spent rounds from the victims and wall surfaces were free of prints and were a mix of common rounds readily available. Most were of an older manufacture, and some appeared to be reloads."

"Reloads?" The ADD raised a brow.

"Our shooter may have done them himself or picked up the ammo in a secondary market. You can buy them by the bag at swap meets and gun shows in the area. The key is that this was a real Chex Mix of ordnance. Impossible to trace back to a source."

"Could this point to a possible militia connection or a white supremacy group?" The ADD set his mug aside and tapped fingers on the desktop.

"That's not apparent," Larry sighed. "My money's on one pissed-off guy. And all the victims were white."

The Bureau and the DoJ had been sex-mad for militias since the 1990s. In recent years, they'd added white supremacy organizations to the list of undesirables that the justice community had convinced itself were roaming the highways and byways committing all manner of racist atrocities that went unpunished. Thousands of man hours that should had been spent pursuing organized criminals, cartel thugs and terrorists were used up chasing rumors of secret armies of troglodyte insurrectionists and race-haters hiding somewhere in the dark heartland of America. Larry thought, hell, he *knew*, this was pure fantasy. Either that or, this enemy within, this viper at the breast of democracy, had been biding their time over his entire career at the FBI and the ten years prior he spent as an ADA in St. Louis. The only hate crime investigations he'd been involved with turned out to be fraudulent, the victim turning out to be the perpetrator in the end.

"Pissed off about what?" the ADD said, deflated.

"There were missing children recovered at the scene. That can't be ignored."

"That wasn't part of your investigation. The Georgia staties are handling that angle, right?"

"Yes, sir."

In fact, that part of the investigation was to be ignored as if it didn't exist. Larry had been directed from the outset to compartmentalize his work to only the shooting incident and attendant evidence. He was not to explore or conflate any evidence dealing with the abducted children found at the crime scene. These kids, all under twelve, were all potential witnesses but Larry wasn't allowed to interview them or even see any statements they might have made to Georgia law enforcement. The entire case was being treated as if the multiple series of capital crimes committed at the Dutton home on New Year's Eve were entirely separate, unrelated incidents.

Anything those kids might have seen or heard would increase the compiled evidence of the shooter's identity by magnitudes. Currently, the only physical evidence that might help were some bloody boot prints that had to belong to the shooter. They were from a brand widely available from a major big box discount store. The shooter wore a size fourteen and that's all they knew of him. From that it could be extrapolated that their suspect was over six foot tall. That narrowed the field to millions.

There was nothing else. No fingerprints. No surveillance videos. The shooter had gotten away without leaving his own blood behind despite evidence that there was copious return fire from his victims. The house was a shooting gallery that night. The neighboring houses heard nothing as they were each close to a hundred yards away and the Dutton home was heavily soundproofed. Even the driveway yielded no joy. It was all gravel and the shooter left behind no tire tracks.

While the ADD entertained daydreams of John Birchers, Klansmen and secret orders of throwbacks and reactionaries as yet unknown, Larry stuck to his "one pissed-off guy" theory. To him, this *had* to be about the kids. Some avenging angel showed up that night, a father or other relative of one of the captive kids,. and cleaned house. Probably took his son, daughter, nephew, or niece away with him, carried them off bodily otherwise there'd be a set of smaller footprints beside the size fourteens. The key to the investigation was those kids. But that avenue was firmly, no-questions-asked, barred to him.

"So," the ADD said with a shrug, "recommendations?"

"We have fourteen dead. A mass shooting. We can continue to look into the associations between the victims."

The ADD wrinkled his nose, his mouth pressed to a tight line.

"In any case, obviously, we'll keep the case in the open file." The ADD gestured at the open folder with his mug. "But, unless fresh evidence lands on our doorstep tomorrow, it looks like we're at a dead end. Am I right?"

"You're probably right, sir."

"Outstanding, Agent Crozier. Excellent work all around." The ADD pushed away from his desk to rise. "Leave the folder with me and tell your section chief you're available for reassignment."

"Yes, sir. Thank you, sir."

And, with that. Larry found himself out in the marble-floored hallway, free of the weight of the work he'd assembled over the last three months and released for new ventures. He stood at the elevators, a sick feeling roiling his stomach. He knew the feeling. It was unfinished business. It was the lack of closure. It was the niggling itch of an unsolved mystery. More than that, it was those kids. Where were they now? Returned to their families? Back in the of the care of the foster system? This whole investigation stank like a mountain of shit, and he'd spent the past weeks adding to its height.

The elevator came and he boarded, joining a pair

of secretaries in conversation about their weekend plans. He made an effort to shift his mind from the slaughter in Georgia, the horror house with its barred windows and closet-like cells. There were eight more months until his twenty. After that he and Laura would cash out of their three bedroom in Arlington and head for the condo in Fort Meyers. He'd have no reason to ever think again of the red house and its grisly contents. He'd never have to think of the victims and how almost all of them raised red flags for past charges and convictions for statutory rape and sexual knowledge of a minor. He'd be free of that.

Like hell I will, he thought as he exited the elevator. His section chief could wait. He was going over to the bar at the Marriott for a double vodka.

4

Phillip Barnes, man of the people and representative of all the hard-working families of Congressional District 10, kept a humble little office in a strip mall between a nail salon and a Hungry Howie's. He also had a humble little three-bedroom house off Sawyer Road where he raised his humble little family. The door to his office was always open to his constituents, as he would often declare when on the stump. And whenever he was on the stump, collecting votes and contributions, that was most certainly true.

But when he was not on the hustings working to secure his next term of office, his twentieth, the congressman spent much of his time at his condo overlooking the Potomac while the House was in session. When it was not in session, he had a rather spectacular place right on the beach in Bimini.

He was only back in Alabama to attend some fundraising events. A few of his larger corporate donors were throwing a wingding and it was the perfect time to shore up relationships, press the flesh and collect a few checks. He needed the support this

LEVON'S PREY | 19

year as there were rumblings of a primary challenge from some businesswoman out of Cullihane. A young black woman who owned a chain of burger joints and checked all the boxes the media loves despite her support of school choice and lower taxes.

Today he was parked in his strip mall office to meet and greet a sad parade of his constituents and listen to their concerns and problems. He hated being in the close confines of the office with its cheap paneled walls covered in framed photos, indoor/outdoor carpeting and the creaky old wooden desk and the squeaky old chair that chaffed his ass. But his voters loved that common-as-dirt shit. He wondered just how dumb folks had to be to fall for this crap every two years. It made him sad that his entire career rested on the immutable fact that half of the population was below average intelligence.

As dreary as it was, the office was preferable to his home where his wife Dolores was playing queen to her court of extended family. A house loaded up with his freeloading in-laws come to mooch off their rich relations every damn time he was in town. He could only keep a tolerant demeanor for just so long around that cloying, bickering, grasping pack of assholes. When the car came to pick him up for his day at the office, he greeted it like Gabriel's trump come to deliver him from the pit.

Now it was late in the day, and he'd finally seen the last of the citizenry off. A handshake, a friendly pat on the back and an assurance that he'd do all he could to address the last visitor's concerns and he was blessedly alone for the first time in hours. He'd sat most of the afternoon nodding sagely and smiling benevolently at their pleas, protestations and testimonies, his mind thousands of miles away lying back on the deck of his house in the islands under a Caribbean sun where he would be in a few days' time as Congress was on a recess.

"Kay, tell Jimmy to bring the car around front," he called as he stood to pull his Burberry coat from the hook on the back of the door.

"One more visitor, sir," Kay's voice called from the outer office/waiting room.

"Shit," the congressman said to himself before re-affixing a rictus grin to his lips and stepping from the office with a hand held out to clasp that of whatever member of the great unwashed had come to seek his council.

"You," he said and lowered his hand.

"Good to see you *too*, your honor," the pale white man said as he stood up from the upholstered benches that lined one wall.

The congressman told Kay to head on home before ushering the visitor into the office. She left without question, anxious to be out of the company of the visitor who'd been staring at her with piggy eyes and creepy smile for the past quarter hour. Phillip Barnes retook his seat behind the desk and the pale man dropped into one of the guest chairs.

Barnes did not like Lew Dollinger. Then again, he liked very few, and admired none, of the many people he had to deal with in his profession. Men like Dollinger were a necessary part of his life, a tool to be used and put aside when the work is done and only to picked up again when another unpleasant task arose. Not that Phillip Barnes had ever done a day's actual work in all his sixty-two years.

"You wanted to see me?" Dollinger said. "I did

the Kingsley thing. That kid of his got game. He pull that bid?"

"This morning. But that's not why I wanted to see you."

"I knew he would. I always know I got to them when I see the sweat in their hairline."

The congressman made to interrupt the man, but the cracker was into his recount, and it was best to allow him to finish.

"Smelled it before I saw it. You know, that nigger smell when they sweat. 'specially when they's scared."

Barnes winced at the unpleasant word. Not that he gave a damn for niggers, coons, jungle bunnies, darkies or coloreds. But because he'd worked so hard over the decades to re-order his mind to remove those terms from even his most private conversations. One overheard remark, a side comment on a hot microphone, and he could kiss his house seat goodbye.

"That's good news," the congressman said. "Well done."

And it *was* good news. Now the bidding on the annex job would come down to Apex Paving, owned by his cousin, or Poundstone Concrete, owned by his brother's eldest son. The kickback from either of them as well as many other family businesses, was what kept up the humble little office, humble little house, residences in Virginia and Bimini and his twice-yearly jaunts to Thailand. Those vacations were enjoyed without the company of Dolores, of course.

"You got something new for me then?" Dollinger asked.

"Associates of mine, associations I do not wish to

be made public, have been having problems lately."

"These, like, legal problems? Or like you need some nosy newspaper man dissuaded from looking further into their affairs?"

"One of them was abducted."

"You mean like kidnapped? You need me as a bagman?"

"This was months ago. I do not expect we will ever see him again."

"Months ago? What's the job then?"

"I need you to find who took him. And I need some things back that his abductors may have taken."

"What kind of things?"

"Personal items."

"Well now, your honor," Dollinger leaned forward in his chair and pulled on his nose, "I appreciate that these are personal and private items, but I need to know a bit more if I'm to look for them."

"I don't know what Hicks had in his possession." Barnes rummaged in the drawer of his desk as he spoke. "Tapes. Discs. Phones. Paper files Anything like that. Any kind of recording device."

"I see. This Hicks is the fella that's gone missing?"

"Taken." The congressman pulled a file from the drawer and pushed it across the desktop at his visitor. "Here's what I have on the abduction. Justin Hicks, an attorney specializing in adoptions. County and state. I might be getting more information. I can't be sure. It's all gone cold."

"I take it the police have lost interest in this case?" Dollinger pursed his lips and leafed through the file. "I don't like being in competition with law enforcement. Puts me in the middle, you understand."

"You won't have any interference. Like I said, it's

cold now."

"There's not much here for me." Dollinger held up the open file. "This'll take some diggin'. I'll need some travelin' cash."

Barnes unlocked a lower drawer to remove a steel box of petty cash. He peeled twenty-one hundred dollar bills off a stack. Eyes on the greenbacks, his visitor tilted his chin up in a reverse nod. The congressman counted off ten more and placed the pile on the desk. Dollinger scooped them up and slipped them into a coat pocket with the grace of a sleight of hand master.

"Can you help me out a *little* bit, your honor? Any personal theories on why anyone would want to abduct this Hicks?" He pronounced it 'ab-duck.'

"He pissed someone off. As I said, I know little of Hicks's associations."

"He's a lawyer," Dollinger said, nodding. "I'll sure have no shortage of possibilities."

"Just find the men who took him and bring what they took to me."

"And what is our attitude toward these abductors?" Ab-duckers.

"Before the month is out, if you can." The congressman stood to gesture toward the door.

5

"Can't decide if I want to go with bottles or jars," Uncle Fern said, head down over an open catalog. "Jars are more traditional."

"For liquor?" Levon said as he buttered a triangle of toast. "Traditional was gallon plastic jugs."

They were sitting opposite one another in a booth having what Fern insisted on calling a "business breakfast" at Fay's, the only eat-in establishment in the blink-and-you-miss-it town of Colby. Cades had eaten there for generations, ever since the original Fay, long since passed, opened it in the 50s. It was a short walk from the new headquarters of Blue Moon Whiskey Inc., now situated in the former Rimes Auto Service garages.

"We can't be shipping in gallons," Fern huffed and flipped to a new page in the supply catalog. "What would people think?"

"I wasn't aware we cared what people think. Only what people drink."

"Smartass."

"All's I know is, Fern, me and Dale spent a lot of

days washing out used milk jugs for my daddy. I never heard that anyone complained about what his corn came in." Dale was Levon's younger brother, also passed as had Levon's father.

"Well, there's a lot to deal with and you haven't been much help at all." Fern used a pen to circle an entry for a sixteen-ounce jar, and folded the corner of the page over.

"I've been a lot of help," Levon said around a mouthful of egg and home fries. "Who hauled those lifts out and patched the cement floor? Who steam-cleaned all the grease out of there? That was a job. I put new fixtures in the rest room and replaced that hot water heater."

"Yeah, yeah." Fern nodded over his catalog.

"Made sure the electric was up to code too. You'd never have passed county inspections without me."

"And I appreciate it, nephew. But I mean like making decisions. Shit, Merry's been more helpful with that than you."

"Like what?"

"Like dealing with all these suppliers. How am I to know I'm not getting ripped off? How do I know I'm paying a higher price than I ought to for containers and cartons and shit like that? There's a lot to consider. You could at least take an interest."

"You're the one wanted to be in business, Fern."

"And *you're* the one *needs* to *be* in business, Levon. Or maybe you plan on telling the taxman you *found* all that money you've been spending?"

Levon conceded his uncle's point by silently chewing a wedge of toast.

"All these unit prices and discounts," Fern said, stabbing a figure at a densely worded page in the catalog illustrated with tables and graphs. "It was easier back when me and your father sold by the gallon out of the trunk of a car."

"It's a lot of math, that's for sure."

"I just don't want to get taken by some shyster."

"They'll see you coming a mile off."

"That's what worries me."

"So, turn it back on them," Levon said, freshening his coffee from a carafe.

"What's that mean?" Fern squinted at him.

"Contact a few of these suppliers you're looking at and ask them for quotes. Then you'll have a ballpark. Use those figures to get them to bid for your business. You're just starting up. They might give you a break to try and keep your business."

"That's not a bad idea," Fern said, closing the thick catalog and setting it with a pile of similar books. "All's I have to do is call them, right?"

"Let them work it out for you and go with the one that's cheapest."

"What about shipping?"

"Same thing, I guess," Levon shrugged. "Packaging too. Make 'em come to you."

"See?" Fern said, reaching across the tabletop to stab a finger into Levon's forearm. "All's I needed was to talk to you. Was that so hard?"

"Tortures of the damned," Levon said and helped himself to a sausage link off his uncle's plate.

Their talk turned to the more trivial with Fern doing most of the talking and Levon studying the light traffic moving along Colby's two-lane main drag. Fay's was empty as it was nearing ten o'clock in the morning. The breakfast rush here was between six and eight. Mostly locals, mostly farmers. The only customers now were a pair of kids agonizing over their choice of doughnuts. The current Fay, granddaughter to the original, waited behind the glass display with the patience of Job, a square of wax paper in her hand.

An old step-sider Chevy pickup pulled into one of the spaces in Fay's postage stamp parking lot. It was a 1960's model but fully restored with gleaming chrome and metal flake paint job. Tinted windows and trailer mirrors. A big old whip antenna looped to a catch on the bed wall bobbed above it as the truck came to stop against the concrete bumper.

A broad shouldered and broad bellied man climbed out of the cab on the driver's side. He wore a polo shirt under a leather car coat. A pale-yellow fishing hat propped atop close-cropped salt and pepper hair. A man in his fifties letting himself go. From the passenger side slipped a thinner version of the man, a before and after picture. This guy was younger by thirty years and also had broad shoulders but was lean and wore black hair to his shoulders. He had on bib overalls over a bare chest and his arms were nearly black from shoulders to wrists with prison ink.

Fern turned to the window, piqued by Levon's interest in the newcomers.

"Shit," Fern said under his breath.

Levon turned to the door as the brass bell hung above it rang. Fern made a hissing noise to get him to turn his eyes back to their booth. The new customers entered Fay's, the older man talking and the younger answering in grunts.

"Well, shit the bed," the older man said as he came level with their booth. "Is that Fernie Cade sittin' there?"

"Hey, Rolly," Fern said, flicking his eyes upward.

"And who's this?" the man said.

"Levon," Levon said, offering his hand.

"Your nephew, Fernie? I remember you runnin' 'round with another kid. Your brother?"

"That was Dale."

"Right," the man said in a long drawl of remembrance. "Two of you always in trouble. Just like my boy here. Deke, say hello."

Deke nodded and grunted, brushing hair from his eyes.

"Well, we was about to get back to work," Fern said. Dropped a twenty for their breakfast by his plate and began to scoot along the booth bench.

"Heard about that," Rolly said, stepping back to allow Fern out. "A legitimate shine business. Goin' into bigtime brewin', that right? Sell lightnin' to hipster assholes in Hollywood."

"Assholes spend money too," Fern said.

Rolly exploded in laughter at that though his eyes remained cool on Fern and Levon. He jabbed an elbow into his son's ribs. Deke was not amused but offered a simpering grin. Rolly kept it up, forcing a chuckle while Fern and Levon made for the door.

"See you later, Hollywood," Rolly called after them.

6

"Son of a bitch," Fern said as he and Levon walked along the cracked asphalt walk that ran along the main road through Colby. Fern had the stack of supplier catalogs under one arm.

"That was Roland Taggart, wasn't it?" Levon said.

"That was him, the son of a bitch."

"You had bad blood with the Taggarts. You and my dad."

"Just a business rivalry," Fern said. "Rolly and his dad worked some thumpers out on a property they had up Westcott way. There was plenty of customers but him and his old man were always trying to steal our accounts."

"He still runnin'?"

"What I heard was he has a half dozen stills goin' year round. Has standing orders with shot houses as far north as Baltimore."

"He had run-ins with the law? Those are convict tats his boy's sporting."

"Naw. Deacon got himself mixed up with some bikers running drugs. Did five years at Parchman

Farm."

"Mississippi?"

"Yeah. Transporting that oxy-cotton out of Biloxi." They crossed the lot to the former Rimes garage. It was newly painted with a fresh coat of whitewash and the doors and trim in blue. An empty space on the wall over the entrance was awaiting the sign men who would paint the Blue Moon logo on the bricks.

"Now he's back home." Levon waited while Fern unlocked the man door that was set beside the garage bays.

"In the family business, I guess," Fern said and let them into the office. It was just an old oaken desk, a pair of chairs and a filing cabinet now. The phone hadn't even been hooked up. The company was coming tomorrow to run in a cable for internet access.

"They gonna be trouble for us?" Levon stepped to the interior window that looked into the garage. Empty now with white-washed walls and a clean concrete floor re-surfaced with a fresh coat of speckled epoxy.

"I don't see why. We're a legal concern. We're priced outside their market. No competition for them from us."

"I don't know. That Rolly seems like the kind to enjoy a pissing contest. I remember my dad talking about him. Not much good to say."

"There wouldn't be," Fern said, taking a seat in the padded swivel chair behind the desk. He spread the catalogs across the desktop. "My brother, your daddy, could be mean as a snake. But he was never any kind of asshole. But Rolly Taggart is a petty, vindictive fat fuck all the way down to the ground. Whatever you heard your daddy say was only half the story."

"He's doing well from the looks of that truck of his."

"Rolly's always done good. His daddy was a dragon or a kleagle or some shit like that back when that still carried weight down at the county seat. Gives him a pass for that rotgut pisswater he bottles."

"Bad stuff?"

"Uses pig shit in his mash to speed up the cook. Man has no sense of quality or pride."

"Well, if that's the case, we have nothing to worry about," Levon said and took the visitor's chair. "He'll work his side of the street and we work ours."

"Let me have your phone and I'll start these folks fighting for our business." Fern waggled fingers over the desktop. Levon hitched up to retrieve his phone from his back pocket.

He walked through the adjoining door into the garage area to leave his uncle to dicker.

The smell of rust and oil was gone, and the space was clean now. Fresh paint and new floor covering. There was a pair of drains in the floor under where each of the copper vats would be set once they came. Levon's task today was to assemble two long steel frame tables that would be used for labeling and packing. There were also shelves to be put together, one to hold cartons of empty bottles and the next to hold filled cases for delivery. There was still a lot to be worked on, but it looked like Fern could be up and cooking before the month was out. That meant orders out the door in a few weeks' time. All that was left after that was to cook up some phony numbers to justify Levon's income. The cash squirreled away in coffee cans and buried all over Fern's farm would be turned into legitimate spending green.

And, who knew for sure, maybe Blue Moon Whiskey could stand on its own.

7

Seth Tyler's leg still ached like a bitch. Especially in the mornings.

He sat up in bed to rub at his thigh, his hands running over the ropey scar tissue left by the sutures. The massage relieved the pain enough to make getting to his feet tolerable. He looked forward to the warmer months. These chill mornings really put the bite on him. Well, afternoons, anyway. The clock by his bed read past two. He pulled on a T-shirt and running pants.

Once again, he thought about relocating further south. Florida or maybe New Orleans. Once again, he cursed the unknown cracker who plowed into the Merc he was driving a few months back. Same cracker fuck took his employer, Mr. Justin Hicks Esq., and neither of them were ever seen again. Cops never knew shit or, more likely, never told him shit.

Kicking discarded laundry aside, Seth limped to the kitchenette of his one-bedroom. He promised Tandy he'd clean up his shit today. This was her place, and she was letting him stay here. Only right he pick up after himself now and then. He started coffee and poured himself a bowl of cornflakes. In the fridge he grabbed a jug of milk and noticed his last banana was gone. That had to be Tandy. Bitch got up early for her shift at UPS and took his last nanner. Least she could have done is let him watch her eat it, he thought with a grin.

The docs at rehab told him the early morning aches were something he'd need to get used to once he was out of traction and the cast came off. The effects of a compound fracture like the one Seth had suffered were serious. They'd reset his bones in a series of surgeries but left the broken leg slightly shorter than it had been before. Nothing could be done about that except for an orthotic lift worn in his shoe. Even with that he still had a bit of a limp. He decided to lean into it and began carrying a walking stick with a brass ball on the end. Tandy took to calling him her Mack Daddy.

At least he was out of the hospital. Three goddamn months with his leg strung up to a pole. His ass hurt from laying in one place for days on end. Bored all the time. Hungry all the time. Horny all the time. And they never sent one of the pretty nurses when it was time for his sponge bath. Some nights it was a male nurse, some queer as fuck motherfucker, offering to soap him up.

And he lost the sweet gig he had with the lawyer. Justin Hicks was gone, vanished from the face of the earth. No lawyer, no job. At least he didn't get his brains blown out like the boss's other bodyguard/go-fer. Seth knew that lawyers made lots of folks angry. But Mr. Hicks helped people adopt kids. Who'd get pissed off about that?

He took his bowl into the living room and flipped on the TV to take his mind from these unanswerable questions while he ate his cereal sans banana and waited for the coffee maker to finish.

A guy in a studio was speaking to some skinny chick standing in an empty sports arena.

The bell at the door rang its two-tone chime.

Probably Amazon. Tandy was constantly ordering shit. Seemed like there was always something coming to the door. And it was his job to get it out of the hallway before one of the other thieving tenants in the building helped themselves to it. He was expecting either the usual chirpy delivery driver or to find a carton with the signature smile logo on it resting against the door.

He opened the door to find some albino cracker was smiling at him.

"You went and got yourself banged up good, son."

"Who the fuck are you?" Seth asked.

"Just come to ask you a few questions, is all." The guy stepped into the apartment, casting creepy blue eyes around.

"Questions about what? You police? Where's your badge?" Seth backed up into the living room.

"Your little accident," the cracker said. "Your boss's abduction." Ab-duck-shun.

"You with the insurance company?"

"I'm with *your* insurance company, son." The cracker took a seat, hipshot, on the arm of a chair.

"Is that so?"

"Oh yeah," the cracker said, helping himself to the remote to turn the TV off. "I'm here to look after you, make sure you don't get hurt anymore."

"I'm already hurt."

"Could always be worse." The cracker reached a long arm out to give Seth a poke in the leg with the remote.

"Hey, watch that."

"A whole lot worse." The cracker poked again.

"Motherfuck—"

Seth pressed a hand to the sofa to rise but found himself pressed back into the cushions. The larger man had a hand to his chest and a knee on his damaged leg. The pain lanced up into his groin bringing tears to his eyes. Seth had been leaned on before and done some leaning himself working collections for a bookie. He'd done gigs as a bouncer before becoming Mr. Hicks's security. He was always able to take care of himself. But this fucker had fifty pounds on him, and the biggest hands Seth had ever seen on a man. The gem on a pinkie ring winked at him from the hand on his chest.

The cracker leaned in close, voice low.

"Why'd someone take your boss-man, son? What'd he do to get someone so riled?"

"I don't know. I just drove for him."

"Bull. Shit. You were his nigger. Your job was to watch over his ass. What kinda trouble was he in he needed some big buck like you playing bodyguard?"

"He was a lawyer, is all."

The cracker put more weight on his knee sending fresh lightning up Seth's leg.

"More bullshit. What kind of lawyer gets himself abducted like that?"

"He helped folks get kids. You know, adoptions."

"Oh, I *bet* he helps folks get kids." Pink lips parted to show nasty tombstone teeth in the cracker's grin. The man leaned closer to fill Seth's nose with the smell of wintergreen and stale cigarettes.

"I don't know his business. Never knew it." Seth looked into the man's pale eyes looking for understanding. All he saw there was a brand of amused contempt.

"*Funny* business. Like those boxes the police found in your boss's car. I talked to that pretty little girl used to work for your boss-man. She didn't know nothing. Was there more of that kind of stuff at the house?" The cracker eased up a bit. Seth sipped in air.

"Mr. Hicks had a safe there. I guess he had more stuff."

"Like what was in the car? What kind of stuff was that?"

"Paper files. Hard drives. Some discs."

"Well, that's real interesting. What's on all them was so important? What's there that someone might want to take a look at?"

"I stay outta all that." Seth ground his teeth, fighting down the pain.

"Well, good for you, son. That's just fine. Only I'm bettin' you took a little peek now and then, didn't you? Like Lot's wife. You got curious and wanted to see what it's all about. Don't lie to me, son. I can *smell* a nigger lie."

"Fuck you." Seth's anger washed away the pain from his leg. This guy was a *real* cracker. An honest-to-goddamn racist motherfucker. The kind of white man his grandma used to tell him about when she talked about nightriders.

"Don't be like that." New weight on the leg. Another flash of pain. Another smile from his visitor. "Tell me about this fella who took your boss-man."

"I never saw him." Seth bit back a groan. "Didn't see shit."

The pressure came off. Seth opened his eyes to see the cracker grinning down at him.

"You rest up here now, son." The cracker gave his face a gentle pat. "Do what the doctor tells you. I might stop by sometime to see you again just to check up on how ya'll are doin'."

And the man was gone.

Seth lay back on the sofa, the cushions beneath him sodden with sweat. His leg throbbed sending aching waves in rhythm with his pulse. He strained to raise himself again, a hand clutching the sofa arm.

8

Lew Dollinger left the gimpy nigger's apartment and shared an elevator to the parking garage with a pair of little snots wearing hospital scrubs under winter jackets. They were both engaged in a lively discussion about some airy-fairy bullshit that was cut to dead silence once he stepped into the car to seemingly take up all the remaining room. Dollinger pressed the button for the garage and watched the floor numbers light up. The silence deepened as they rode down, the two scrubs looking to one another with mute expressions. He startled them by turning to speak to them directly.

"You boys hear about the fire at the circus?" he said.

"Was that on the news?" one of the scrubs said, the other just staring.

"The heat was in tents," Dollinger said with a crooked smile revealing brilliant acrylic teeth.

To the pair of interns, the next twenty seconds before the elevator doors opened with a ding seemed like an eternity.

"Intense. Get it?" Dollinger called after their retreating backs as they scurried away across the building's lobby.

"Faggots," he said to himself.

He continued on down to the garage and walked to his car. Dollinger eased his big frame into the front seat of a '90 Cadillac Brougham and punched in the lighter. He'd bought it at a police auction a few years back. A real relic and his baby. His cousin rebuilt it for him and fitted it with big 350, heavy duty shocks and an exhaust system that sounded like a lion's purr. Gave it an eight-coat paint job in deep metallic blue and re-chromed the bumpers and trim. It suited him. A large car for a large man.

He sat a moment, allowing the car to warm up as he twiddled scarred fingers atop the steering wheel. His pinky ring tapped time to George Strait coming out of the radio. The lighter popped out and he used it to start up a Hav-A-Tampa. He blew azure smoke across the dash.

Two days working this case and he had jack shit to show for it. He enjoyed talking to the lawyer's pretty, little secretary, only she was as ignorant of Mr. Justin Hicks's business as was the nigger in the room upstairs. He wanted to talk to the lawyer's daughter only she'd gone off to stay with relatives. The big old house out in Owens Cross sat empty now. She probably didn't know much anyway. Kids today weren't family close like in his day. Kin lived like strangers anymore, even under the same roof.

The police files were as useless as tits on a wheelbarrow. Only he knew that cops never put down in reports every single thing *they* knew or saw. There might be something in talking to the deputies who reported to the Hicks house and to the hit-and-run. He had the names of the officers on the reports, and he knew where most of the deputies went to drink when they came off shift. Maybe buy a few rounds and see what he could learn.

He gunned the Caddy to life and started down the ramp to the street, cracking the window to let cigarillo smoke bleed out into the cold evening air.

***

Round after round of drinks at Harley's, a shithole faux pub that occupied the end of a sad strip mall on Pratt. It was a hangout for off-duty local cops and deputies. Not the kind of place Lew Dollinger would frequent if it weren't for business. The bar was hung with green tinsel and shamrocks for the upcoming St. Paddy's Day. The jukebox was playing some candyass country pop, the girl singing sounding like a horny chipmunk. Two familiar faces were holding down one end of the bar, a pair of retired Huntsville PD bulls he'd had business with a time or two. Otherwise, the rest of the customers were either civilians or uniforms unknown to him.

"Something goin' on? This place used to hop after shift change," Dollinger asked once the re-introductions had been made. Only a few booths were occupied and, except for himself and the two old bulls, the bar was unoccupied.

"New guys. They go straight home to their families. Only ones here are the single guys and divorces," one of the bulls said. His buddy grunted agreement.

He'd been in the wars with these two old boys back in the day. Years before when he'd run some off-the-books operations for local businesses and, a few times, for the mayor. He was doing the same thing then he was doing now, fixing problems and smoothing the road for the powers that was. Sometimes he'd spread a little cash around to off-duty cops to help with getting some miscreant's mind right or run some bum out of town. This was another time before the world got taken over by the pussies. The talents of men like Lew Dollinger were no longer appreciated unless and until someone got into the shit up to their lower lip as the honorable Congressman Phillip Barnes had apparently done.

"Different world," Dollinger said. "I 'member nights in here when half the cops was busy arrestin' the other half."

"We tore it up in our day." Another grunt from his buddy.

"When it was still all right to be a white man," Dollinger said with a snort and reached out his shot glass to clink the necks of the others' tallboys.

He let the evening go on and things unwound a bit before he offered to pick up the tab for a booth full of what turned out to be deputies. They weren't sure of who exactly this big albino was but the two old heads at the bar seemed to know him, and he was paying. He started with generalities then worked his way around to his point, the kidnapping and homicide earlier in the year. Beers, bourbons and a few rounds of wings and hushpuppies later and it turned out none of them knew much about the Hicks abduction other than the fact that the feds had come in and claimed the case for themselves.

"Your department even close to a suspect?" Dollinger asked.

"Some white guy in a pickup," a deputy, a spic, half-shot on drinks paid for by Dollinger, slurred.

"With that description you could fill the Von Braun with possibles," another deputy, a high yellow, chimed in.

"There's nobody working this local?"

"Not unless the feds call on us to knock on some doors, which they ain't done," the spic said.

"Someone grabbed a lawyer. Fuck 'im." The high yellow raised a Michelob.

The subject turned away toward basketball. Dollinger dropped a few bills on the table to cover the last round and pushed away. He made to wave to the two old bulls at the bar, but they were no longer there. He'd paid a two-hundred-dollar bar tab out of the kitty the congressman had given him and had nothing to show for it.

A cold drizzle turned the pole lamps on the strip mall lot to halos. He hunched his shoulders against the chill and trotted for the Caddy. On the radio, Jessi Colter sang a plaintive song of loss and longing that matched his mood as he drove the rain-shiny streets to his place in Shady Lane.

Two days on the hunt and no luck to be found. Not even a whiff of promise. There were other cop bars he could visit but that would only be good money after bad. With the FBI on the case, everything would be locked up tighter than a tick's cornhole. Even if he were to take a trip to the nation's capital, there wasn't a big enough bar tab in the world to get any of those career assholes to share with him. That left him to hunt down this phantom white guy all on his own. He drove the winter streets in a bleak mood that had not been the least bit improved by a half dozen shots of Maker's he'd downed.

Dollinger pulled the Caddy into a spot before his building and made his way to the two-bedroom on the ground level with nothing more to look forward to than falling asleep in front of the TV.

An envelope with the colorful markings of a delivery service rested on the mat before his door. He stooped to pick it up. There was no return address on the label other than "HNTSVLL, AL."

Inside his place, he snapped on the kitchen lights to take a stool at the counter and open the package.

There was no note attached to the paper file within the package. The file contained a print-out of a surveillance photo that showed a pickup truck crossing an intersection. It was a Chevy Avalanche in a dark color that was hard to pin down due to the poor quality of the photo. A copy of a copy. There was a time stamp and location still clear across the bottom of the photo.

He nuked a mug of water to pour in some Folger's crystals. He had the police reports papers still sorted out atop his kitchen table. Sipping the strong coffee to clear his mind, he compared the photo of the truck to the reports of deputies who responded to the hit-and-run.

Northwood and Sparkman in Brookhurst at 10:07 a.m. Just after the time of the hit and run. The truck was heading east on Sparkman.

The photo fit the timeline and location.

Hunting through a drawer in the kitchen, he came up with a city map and unfolded it flat atop the table. His finger traced Sparkman west back to near the office park where Hicks's car got totaled and the lawyer got himself taken. The first deputies were on the scene by 10:18.

His finger followed Sparkman east to surface roads that allowed access to Memorial Parkway that ran north and south. Further east it joined State Road 2 that ran roughly north/northeast to Chattanooga. Those were the two likely getaway routes. Either would have taken the truck far from the grab site within minutes.

Somewhere along all those miles of highway there had to be another camera that picked up the Avalanche.

It wasn't much. But it was a place to start.

9

"What do you think?" Merry said, moving her head aside so the screen of her laptop would be visible.

"I like it," Hope said, raising up on her tiptoes to lean over Merry's shoulder to squint.

On the screen was the highly stylized logo for Blue Moon Whiskey. Inside a circle was a full moon in pale blue against an indigo sky. The silhouette of a wooded ridgeline of pines set against the moon's glow.

"I think maybe you might need glasses," Merry said.

"I see fine," Hope protested.

"I guess you can see anything you want to as long as you can touch it with your nose."

Hope offered Merry's head a playful slap which the older girl ducked with ease.

"Come on, I need constructive criticism," Merry said, catching Hope's wrist before she could land a second attempt. "And if you wore glasses you could probably make one of those slaps sting."

"I think it's good," Hope said, returning her gaze

to the screen. "But why is it a blue moon?"

"Like people say, 'once in a blue moon.'"

"Like 'once upon a time'?"

"No, like something that doesn't happen very often. Something rare."

Merry returned her attention to the program she was using to design the logo for her dad and uncle's company. It was practically the only work she'd be allowed to do for them until she was of legal drinking age. She tweaked the color of the tree line in the foreground. The men were coming in a few days to paint the logo on the wall of the distillery building in Colby.

"'A seasonal blue moon is the third full moon of an astronomical season that has four full moons,'" Hope read from the screen of her phone. "'A monthly blue moon is the second full moon in a calendar month with two full moons.'"

"And how often does that happen?"

"Um, it looks like it happens once every three years." Hope slid her thumb across the screen, the phone held close to her face.

"See? Something you don't see every day. Something rare."

Merry clicked the mouse to save her work and closed the laptop. She leapt from her chair to move across the room they shared. When she was ten feet from Hope she held up three fingers.

"How many fingers am I holding up?"

Hope squinted hard, her dark eyes turning to slits.

"Oh my God, Hopey!" Merry barked. "You're blind as a bat!"

"Why are you being mean to me?" Hope's features darkened.

"I'm not being mean. You need glasses. Why'nt you tell us you were having trouble?"

Hope turned away to throw herself belly first on her bed.

"Glasses are ugly."

"No, they're not! Felicity on *Arrow* wears glasses and you always say how cute she is. And Mrs. Grimes at the school wears them too and she's the prettiest teacher we have."

"I do not want Daddy to spend the money. He has spent so much for me."

"Well, it'd cost a lot more if you walked in front of a truck or fell down a well because you can't see for crap!"

"You talk as if I were blind!"

"Blind as a bat!"

"I am not!"

"Blind as *two* bats!"

"I could hear you girls arguing over the television," Uncle Fern said from the doorway to the girls' room.

"Hope needs glasses!" Merry said and leapt aside to duck a stuffed animal flung her way from Hope's bed. A teddy bear in a tiny Crimson Tide starter jacket.

"See? She missed me by a mile!" Merry crowed.

"I could take you over to Haley tomorrow or the next day," Fern said. "They have a LensCrafters there. That's where I get my specs."

"You could even get contact lenses if you don't like glasses," Merry offered.

"And we could stop by Brewster's for cones after," Fern said, sweetening the deal.

Hope dropped her next missile, a throw pillow, to the bed with a demure nod.

***

"These aren't so bad," Hope said, admiring herself in glass by the serving window at Brewster's.

"Everyone looks cool in sunglasses," Merry said.

"Those are just 'cause they dilated your eyes, Hope," Fern said as he handed each girl a cone. "Your real glasses won't be in until next week."

"You sure you like the pair you picked out?" Merry asked.

"They're just like Felicity's," Hope replied with an emphatic nod.

The girls walked to Fern's truck to each take a seat on the bumper to enjoy their cones. After fumbling one-handed with his wallet to pay for the ice cream, Fern joined them. He handed out napkins before leaning against the fender with his double dip of rum raisin.

"When will you start brewing, Uncle Fern?" Merry asked.

"Well, they promised me the thumpers for next week," Fern replied.

"Thumpers?" Hope said, her upper lip rimed with a green mustache of mint chocolate chip.

"Those are the copper vats I'll use to ferment my mash," Fern said. "Big old tubs. The heart of any still."

"You decided on what you'll use for mash?" Merry asked.

"Apples. Or maybe potatoes. Depends on what I

can get for a good price."

"Does it make a difference to the taste which one you use?"

"Well, Merry, there's folks that say it does. Same kind of folks say there's a difference in how wines or cigars taste. But I think that's all bullcrap."

"Like Coke or Pepsi."

"Just like that. The best shine has a clean taste like a sweet fire. Kind of hard to define."

"Sounds like there's a real science to it."

"I guess. One thing's for sure, it's a lot of work," Fern said, taking a bite from the crumbling edge of his waffle cone.

"You're gonna need help."

"Maybe we could help, huh?" Hope said.

"Naw. The law say you need to be twenty-one to work anywhere near liquor. Serving it or selling it or even making it."

"Who's gonna help you?" Merry said. "It sure won't be Daddy. He doesn't seem so interested in Blue Moon Whiskey."

"Your daddy told me he knows someone might want to work for me."

"Yeah?" Merry's interest was piqued.

"A friend of his."

Merry and Hope exchanged a glance and shared shrug.

"Daddy has a friend?" Merry said, eyes narrowed, and head canted. "When did this happen?"

"Don't know. He just said he knew a fella he might be able to talk into coming on."

"This fella have a name?"

"Don't know his name. Levon never mentioned it."

"Can we see this place?" Hope said, turning her head to avoid the damp napkin Merry was dabbing at her mouth.

"Can we? You're not brewing yet."

"It's an empty building is all, girls. All's there is the cases of glass jars I got delivered and some work tables."

"But once you're cooking, we won't be allowed to visit," Merry said.

"And it's on the way home," Hope said.

"I guess it'd be okay," Fern relented. "Finish your cones and wash your hands and we'll stop in Colby on the way back."

It was coming on dark when Fern pulled the F-150 onto the Blue Moon lot. His headlights played across the front of the building as he swung the front end into a parking slot. In the momentary glare he saw that the man door set in one of the big pull-up garage doors was ajar.

"You girls wait here," he said as he stepped from the cab, the engine still running.

"Something wrong, Uncle Fern?" Merry asked.

"Just lock up after me," he said and drew a ball bat from behind the bench seat before closing the driver side door.

The girls watched him cross the headlight beams and head for the man door to push it open, the slugger held in one fist.

It was dark inside the garage and a sharp stink hung in the air. A stink he knew well. Fern might have thought a wild pig had broken into the garage if it weren't that the padlock and hasp had been pulled free from the door. Freshly scarred metal from where a pry bar had been worked behind the hasp gleamed in the harsh glare of his high beams.

Glass crunched underfoot as he stepped inside. Holding the bat ready to swing at anyone or anything that might come within reach, he crab-walked toward the light switches on one wall of the garage. His booted foot squelched into something wet and sticky as he moved. Uttering a stream of curses under his breath, he snapped on the lights.

Where that morning there were orderly stacks was now an untidy heap of crushed cartons. The floor was carpeted with the silvery shards of over a thousand shattered jars. In addition to the mess of glass and cardboard, the entire place had been liberally splashed with bucket loads of pig shit and urine. The buckets, still crusted with drying feces, lay in a puddle on the floor. They'd made a job of it. Brownish green swaths of the muck rose as high as the ceiling on all the walls.

"Woo. That stinks," Merry said from the doorway. Hope was behind her, nose wrinkled.

"I told you both to stay in the truck," he growled even though he knew whoever'd done this was long gone. Either that or seated somewhere out in the dark amusing themselves by watching the show.

"We got worried about you," Merry said. Fern noted a long-handled wrench his niece held against her leg. She was a Cade, all right.

"Who would do this?" Hope said, covering her nose with her hand.

"I don't know," Fern huffed. "But I got a pretty damned good idea."

10

Lew Dollinger counted twenties out on the table under the hungry eyes of Gage and the big dummy Gage had brought with him.

Gage was a second cousin on his sister's side who referred to himself as a mixed martial arts fighter though he was more of a freelance bouncer. The boy had dreams of grandeur that turned to delusion as he entered his thirties with zero wins at local competitions and toughman contests.

The man mountain who'd accompanied him went by the name Bear and it was apt. It was seldom that Dollinger, a big man himself, was impressed by another man's size. This Bear fella was six foot six and topped out at over three hundred pounds. From the cow-like look in his eyes it didn't appear that brains added much to that weight.

"Looks like a war room, cousin," Gage nodded at the Huntsville area roadmap that was unfolded and tacked to the wall of the dining room. It was marked up with lines and circles and Post-Its handwritten with times like 10:24 and 10:41.

"I'm givin' you both two hundred here," Dollinger held out the stacks of bills for the men and then a handwritten sheet torn from a legal pad for each. "These here are lists of routes and times. The times are pure guesses. You boys will ride north on Memorial and east on Route 2 starting at Sparkman in Brookhurst."

"You want us to split up?" Gage asked, studying his sheet with a squint.

"That's why I asked you to come here in separate vehicles." Jesus, they raise them slow in the family his sister married into, Dollinger thought.

"You want us to talk to folks?" Bear asked in a sleepy voice.

"Not just any folks. I need you to stop anywhere that might have a camera outside at a gas pump or on a store front. You ask real nice if you can look at camera footage from three months ago around the dates and times written on these sheets and on the maps I'm gonna give you."

"What we lookin' for?" Gage asked.

"This truck." Dollinger handed them copies of the stop light cam. "I'm lookin' for a clear angle on the license plate."

"What if they don't take to us talking real nice?" Bear asked.

"Then you offer them some cash. Twenty or forty bucks. Most of these losers working counters at gas and go's will jump at that."

"And if they don't go for sweet talk or cash?" Gage asked.

"Then you get real persuasive," Dollinger said, and the boys nodded. "And don't get real generous with that money. I'm expectin' change."

"What's our end of this?" Gage asked.

"I'll pay two hundred for the day. Four hundred to the man gets me a license plate I can read."

"You payin' for lunch?" This from Bear.

"Hell, boy. Buyin' *you* lunch would break my budget," Dollinger smiled as he said it and the big dummy took it as a compliment. Like being born huge and ugly was some kind of accomplishment to be proud of.

"What's this fella done, cuz?" Gage asked.

"He crossed the wrong people. We find him and there might be another payday in it for you two." Dollinger slipped into his leather coat.

He made sure they had their maps and lists and the number of one of his cells and showed them to the door. He walked them out to the parking lot where they each climbed into their own knobby-tired redneck war machines while he slid into his baby. The trucks roared to life with a thunder he could feel through the floor of his Caddy. Bear gave a grin and wave from the open window of his cab as he backed out with a jerk and a squeal into a thick white cloud of exhaust.

"Like a kid goin' to his grandma's for birthday cake," Dollinger said to himself through a returned smile of gritted teeth. "Fell out the stupid tree and hit every branch on the way down."

***

It was a long but rewarding day.

They met at a Waffle House somewhere close to eleven that night.

As unlikely as it was, it turned out to be Bear who struck gold. Dollinger was happy to treat him to two

All-Star Specials, a hashbrown bowl and a side of sliced ham.

A surveillance camera set under the portico over the pump island at a RaceTrac at Limestone Road in Hazel Green. It was a brand-new store with a hi-def system. A shot of the cars at the pumps was angled to capture part of an intersection of Memorial. A northbound Avalanche was captured in crystal clear 1080 dpi inside the window at 10:42 am.

"Real pretty girl helped me," Bear said around a mouthful. "Didn't want no money for it. Thought I was a detective."

"A dick-tective, more like it," Gage said with a simper.

"These are good, Bear. You done good." Dollinger studied the image on Bear's phone. The truck was the right color and within the right time frame. Alabama plates with clear numbers and letters in black against a green background depicting mountains.

"Got another one here earlier." Bear plucked the phone from Dollinger's hand with a greasy paw. He ran thick gorilla fingers down the screen to scroll along to the image he wanted.

Another shot of the Avalanche time stamped twenty minutes later and taken from the lot of a Dollar Barn. This one was fuzzier and taken as the truck approached a stop light behind a semi-trailer. Despite the poorer quality it was easy to see the damage to the front end. The nose of the hood cover was crumpled and the headlight and running light on one side was out.

"Damn, that's good, boy."

Dollinger scrolled back to the first picture past other images on Bear's phone. Lots of shots of

Bear's truck, Bear at the gym and a buck-toothed girl pulling up her shirt to show off a proud pair of titties.

"Pretty gal," he said as he copied the license number down on the edge of the paper placemat.

"That's Jalene. We was set to get married, then her dad talked her into joining the Air Force," Bear said, face dropping into the solemn expression of a crestfallen ape.

"Women," Gage simpered again.

"All right. Pony up." Dollinger waggled fingers at them. "I said I wanted change."

Bear handed over one-eighty. The shot at the Dollar Barn cost him a twenty. Gage's stack was lighter. Only sixty.

"What the hell?" Dollinger said.

"Some A-rab sumbitch held me up for a hundred, cousin," Gage shrugged. "You know how those fuckers are. Cheaper than Jews and that's the truth. Turned out all his cameras was set wrong anyhow."

"I'll let it go," Dollinger said, eyes hard on his cousin-in-law, letting Gage know he knew the story about the Arab storeowner was pure, thoroughbred horseshit.

The fleeting smile at the corner of Gage's lips confirmed that the little pissant was holding out. Dollinger would let it drop. He'd got what he was looking for after a fruitless day riding south and pestering counter jockeys.

"Anything else for us, Lewis?" Gage said.

"Maybe. Maybe not." Dollinger stirred his coffee and studied the plate number. "I'll know more when I find out where all this takes me."

11

The Avanti Evo made a lazy circle around South
Bimini Island through a cloudless azure sky. It
dropped down to land on the single runway of the
airport and taxied closer to the terminal, a long
metal-roofed structure of cinder block painted a
chalky blue.

It was met by baggage handlers and a customs
officer as the twin props flared to a stop. It off-
loaded a half dozen Americans, couples mostly, here
to enjoy Bahamian days and nights over the Easter
break. The customs man, in his starched white shirt
and crisply pleated shorts, led the vacationers to his
hut where he politely asked them to stand in line and
present their passports.

A young woman, a girl really, stood out from
the rest because she traveled alone. She was also
remarkable for her efforts to look older than she
obviously was. Platform sandals added to her height.
Large-lensed sunglasses and a broad-brimmed straw
hat concealed her features. But her tailored slacks
and batik blouse tied across her midriff did little to

hide her narrow hips, flat chest and coltish legs.

The customs man regarded her with suspicion as he opened her passport.

Her photo in the passport betrayed her age. It showed a fresh-faced young girl with dark brunette hair framing a face that would have been pretty if not for the shining bars of braces visible in her smile. The customs man looked up at her. The braces were gone now leaving only a lovely set of very straight, very white teeth between painted lips. Her hair was also longer than in her photo, hanging in tresses that touched her shoulders.

The name on the passport was Virginia Lea Blossom. Her birthdate set her age at fourteen. Her home address was in Gadsen, Alabama.

"What is your destination here on the island, young lady?"

"I'm staying with my uncle. He has a house in Sampson's Ridge."

"Is your uncle here now?"

"No. He's a very busy man. He told me to go on ahead and he'd be here later today or tomorrow."

"And what is your uncle's name, if you please."

"Phillip Barnes. He's my mother's brother." She said this last as if it were an important detail to impart.

The customs man fought to keep a straight face as he stamped and returned the passport to the girl's manicured fingers. This was not the first of Mr. Barnes's nieces he had encountered. Apparently, Mr. Barnes often shared his island home with many of his young relations, always female. One might be tempted to read unwelcome connotations into the habits of the white-haired old man. But the kind and substantial gifts the congressman shared with the island's customs and immigration officers each Christmas were enough to convince all involved that Mr. Barnes's motives were pure and done out of kindness and generosity only. Such was the nature of the man.

"Enjoy your stay, Miss Virginia." The customs man beamed at her as she took the folder from him.

"You can call me Gina," she said with a shy smile before turning to walk to the car waiting to take her to the house off Port Royale Road.

12

"It was the Taggarts, Levon," Fern growled. The knuckles on his fisted hands turned white.

"You're shaking the ladder," Levon replied from his perch on the top rung. He was screwing a camera in place.

"Sorry. I just get so damned pissed off when I think of that asshole Rolly."

"I could tell."

"Our insurance policy doesn't start until the end of the month. We're on the hook for all that glass. It needs to be replaced. And your girls worked so hard to clean the place up."

"Uh huh."

"We're just damned lucky the vats weren't delivered yet. That would have got expensive."

"You're right."

"We need to do something. Payback is a bitch."

"Hold on," Levon said with a sigh.

He secured the last screw in place under the eave above the garage doors. The camera would cover both entry doors and most of the lot. He had a second camera above the office window that would show the faces of anyone approaching the building. A third was mounted at the rear of the building to keep an eye on the service alley and the steel door there. They were all hi-res and would allow them to read license plates and identify visitors, invited and not, in any light. He climbed down the ladder and handed the cordless drill to his uncle.

"Okay, the whole perimeter is covered. We can check on the place on our phones any time we like. I installed contact alarms on the doors and windows. And a motion detector inside. Anyone breaks in now, we have their ID and the deputies will show up before they can do any serious damage."

"I'm not talking about if they come back again," Fern huffed. "I want to know what we're gonna do about this."

"You're not even sure it was Rolly," Levon said as he drew the extension of the ladder downward. "Could have been some kids."

"It wasn't kids. Kids! What kids? It was Taggart and he wanted me to know it was him. Pig shit everywhere!"

"The Taggarts like pig shit?"

"They *keep* pigs, Levon! Everybody knows Rolly uses hog shit to stoke his mash to ferment. I told you that. All them Taggarts use shit in their thumpers going all the way back."

"That's just a story folks tell."

"A story that's gospel!" Fern was fuming as he followed his nephew to the back of the Avalanche where a toolbox sat open on the tailgate.

"Let's say it was Rolly Taggart done this. Or more likely that retard son of his. Are you going to go to war over it?"

"I don't get mad. I get even."

"I forgot. The family crest." Levon wore the ghost of a smile as he took the Hilti from Fern's hands to remove the screw bit.

"They got to pay. To learn we're not to be fucked with."

"Chances are, if this was the Taggarts, it was a goof. They got drunk and fucked up our place. It's like you said before, Rolly doesn't see you as competition."

"You can't know that." Fern leaned on the side of the truck bed, his big, calloused hands flexing, his eyes hard.

Levon nodded once. The old man was not going to let this go.

"You win," he said, putting the toolbox back in place against the bed wall and securing the rear tonneau panel in place.

"We gonna kick some ass?" Fern's eyes brightened.

"I'm gonna go talk to Rolly."

"Talk to him?" Fern's brows wrinkled.

"See what he has to say." Levon shrugged. "See if there's a way to avoid any more trouble."

Fern didn't answer. He only shook his head, eyes lowered, and lips pressed tight as though to hold back his thoughts.

"We don't need a feud to start out this business," Levon said to his uncle's back as Fern walked forward to open the cab door and climb into the passenger seat without a word in reply.

"You know I'm talking sense," Levon called as he raised the tailgate.

Through the rear cab window Levon saw a stiff

middle finger raised. The radio snapped on and Merle Haggard drawled and twanged through the open cab window. *The Fightin' Side of Me.*

It was going to be a long ride home.

13

Dollinger dropped a fifty on a guy he knew who worked at an auto title company. The guy confirmed the ownership of the Avalanche captured in the camera by the RaceTrac.

The truck was registered to a George Martin Cade. The address was up in the next county north of Huntsville. It was some rural route that showed up on MapQuest as a switchback road which circled back to the county road after snaking through twenty miles of ravines and hollers. The road surface would be for shit. No way in hell he was taking the Caddy up a backwoods goat path like that.

The satellite image showed a one-lane ribbon of road leading off to end at a metal-roofed cabin and some outbuildings. There was a pickup in the yard between the cabin and a barn building. An older model. Not the Avalanche.

No telling when the sat picture was taken. Could be years old. Could even be the truck registration was a fake. Could be the big cracker he was looking for only used this George Cade's name for the plates. Or the truck was stolen. Or maybe they were related somehow. Hell, everybody up in those hills was related somehow. He knew a hillbilly once whose wife was his cousin and his aunt all at the same time.

Dollinger searched the name of George Martin Cade with an Alabama residence. He scrolled past a pediatrician in Selma and a florist in Birmingham before landing on the man he wanted. There wasn't much on the guy but what there was told Dollinger that this wasn't his man. George Cade was seventy-two with a criminal record for illegal distillation of grain spirits back forty years before. It was a state beef both times he was busted, and he did six months at Limestone Correctional each time. That part of the state, a jolt at Limestone was like graduating high school. More frequent, probably.

Nothing much else but a search of the county tax rolls turned up that Cade paid up his property taxes awhile back after five years in arrears and liens stacked to the ceiling. All paid up in one go. And his assessment went up shortly after that with some improvements made to the property. A couple of new outbuildings including a machine shop and a stable. Two acres were fenced in now. Those changes didn't show on MapQuest.

The old guy appeared to be living off a military pension and social security. No sign from what direction any sudden windfalls had blown his way.

He knew a good old gal who worked at Farm Bureau underwriting insurance policies. He gave her a call.

"You know who this is, girl?"

"Can't be Lewis Dollinger 'cause he promised to call me someday." She sounded annoyed but he knew she was playing.

"Well, someday is today, honey-pie."

"After near a goddamn year, is all."

"I think about you every day. Every blessed day."

"What do you want?" She dropped all pretense with a sigh.

"Got a credit history I need a look at."

"And what's in it for me?"

"I'll come around and take you out to dinner. How's that?"

"A real, sit-down restaurant. No drive-through then a trip back to your place."

"Olive Garden. Red Lobster. Whatever you want, babycakes."

"And a hundred dollars."

Fucking bitch. Dollinger strained hard to put a smile in his voice.

"And a dozen roses. Anything for you, girl."

"Give me the name. When I see an Amazon gift card in my email, I'll look it up for you."

"That's my baby," he said through gritted teeth.

She was back in an hour with a full credit history. Cade's rating was in the basement until sometime two years back. Now he had a primo rating. All bills paid, no liens. Not even a mortgage or a car loan despite the Avalanche being a recent purchase. There was a recent application for a business loan. The most interesting aspect of that was the presence of a co-signer.

Someone named Levon Cade.

***

A cousin on his daddy's side owned a used car lot up in Hazel Green. It was two acres of dead grass with loops of faded plastic pennants hanging over three rows of cars and trucks Lonnie picked up at sheriff's auctions for pennies on the dollar. All heavily simonized and the tires liberally sprayed with Armor All like lipstick on a sow.

"You finally lookin' to trade in that Caddy?" Lonnie asked, stepping from the dealer shack.

"Alla these beaters put together wouldn't match Baby's blue book value," Dollinger said as he unhooked the hood release of an '08 F-150. "Besides, I'm gonna be *buried* in that car."

"Like a Viking funeral," Lonnie said and spit a stream of Skoal into the grass.

"Just like that. How 'bout you let me have the loan of this Ford for the rest of the day?"

"In exchange for what?"

"A hundred and I'll fill the tank before I bring her back."

"Sure. You leavin' the Caddy here?"

"Like collateral. I don't come back, she's yours."

"For *my* Viking funeral." Lonnie grinned, showing brown teeth.

"And I know the number on the odometer like I know my psalms." Dollinger did not return his cousin's grin.

"Why you want that old piece of shit? I got better lookin' trucks on the lot."

"Protective coloration, cousin."

"Like cam-o-flage." Lonnie nodded. Eyes narrowed.

"Just like that," Dollinger said. "Get me the keys to this piece of shit. I got places to be."

14

Going up Silver Creek Holler to brace the Taggarts in their lair was a loser strategy. That place would have as much available ordnance as a Taliban refuge. In addition, there would be a pack of attack dogs to tear intruders to chunks and a pen of hogs to eat anything that remained.

Levon figured the Taggarts for creatures of habit. All he'd need to do is sit by the watering hole until one of them showed up.

Deacon Taggart, alone this time, angled a lime green muscle car into a space in front of Fay's. The daily donut run. He climbed out to find Levon approaching him from the Avalanche pulled in a few spaces along.

"You got something to say to me?" Deke barked. His hand went inside the front of his overalls.

Levon crossed the space between them in two strides. Deke stumbled back against the quarter panel of his Charger, eyes on the man closing on him. Levon got an iron grip on Deke's wrist and held his hand there, trapped inside the crotch of the overalls. Deke stared, wild-eyed.

"You gonna let go of that piece or shoot your cock off?" Levon said, his face inches from Deke's.

Levon felt the wrist muscles in his grip relax. There was a metallic clatter on the asphalt as a pretty, little chrome plated automatic dropped from the bottom of Deke's pant leg. Levon drove Deke back against the hood of the car. With one motion, he stooped to snatch up the pistol and flung it, underhand, up onto the flat tar roof of Fay's.

Deke was up off the Charger's hood to take a swing that Levon easily side-stepped. A tap with the flat of his hand to Deke's shoulder sent the man sprawling, belly down, to the sidewalk. Silvery gleams of crushed glass ground into the soles of Deke's Wolverines caught the mid-morning sun.

"Doughnuts are on me this morning," Levon said. He helped Deke to his feet and shoved him toward Fay's door.

Two old timers in a window booth did their best to pretend they hadn't seen the one-sided scuffle outside. Young Fay wasn't so circumspect as she set down fresh coffees before them.

"Don't even think you're getting that gun back, Deacon," she said before turning to folding doughnut boxes together.

"The man wants a mixed dozen," Levon said, taking his mug by the handle and drawing it to him. "It's on me."

"What're you riding me about, Levon?" Deke's habitual sullen attitude had returned though brittle around the edges now.

"It was you busted up my uncle's place."

Deke made to protest. Levon held up a palm.

"I don't know if your daddy told you to or if you just got drunk and decided to be a jackass," Levon said, voice even. "All's I'm saying is, it's gotta stop there."

"Or what?" Deke squinted his eyes in a feeble attempt to restore his manhood.

"Or I come back at you."

"That a threat, Levon?"

"More like a prophecy."

Deke's eyes clouded over as he struggled to find the distinction between the two words.

"Look, you back off and we'll call it bygones. But if you don't, Fern's gonna want to go Vietnam on your asses. And I won't see him hurt. You hear me?"

"What if I don't?" Deke sniffed.

"Then your daddy's gonna blame you for the shit that will rain down if this blows up into a real feud."

Deke blanched at that, his hand shaking where a finger was looped through his mug. A bit of scalding coffee slopped onto his wrist, and he yanked his hand back. That was all Levon need to confirm that Deke acted alone, or with a couple of his asshole buddies. Rolly Taggart knew nothing about any of this.

"Anything he wants that this'll buy," Levon laid a twenty on the counter and set another by it, "and this is for you, Fay, for the use of the room."

Fay swept up the bills and watched Levon step to the street. The two old duffers in the booth stopped their eavesdropping to engage in a muttering conversation.

"Fay…" Deke began.

"That pistol stays up there until Judgment Day, Deacon Taggart," she said, dumping Levon's untasted mug in the sink.

"But…" Deke's voice rose to a whine.

"Else I'll call the deputies and tell them how it happened to get up there."

Deke slumped over his coffee, checkmated.

"Now, what you want for your daddy?" she said, leaning on the counter wearing a professional smile that did not reach as far as her eyes. "We all out of Dutch apple and rainbow sprinkles."

15

The F-150 was limited to an AM/FM radio with only
one speaker left operative. He found a country oldies
station to listen to most of the way. With his pinky
ring tapping on the steering wheel, he kept time
with Willie Nelson, Patsy Cline and Alan Jackson.
Though he took issue with considering Jackson to
be an 'oldie'.

Dollinger took the interstate north to the Haley
exit just shy of the Tennessee border. He followed
a state road west a while before hooking south on a
county road. Once off the county strip he entered a
serpentine labyrinth of what were less like roads and
more like trails. Mostly one lane, with occasional
pull-off areas along either shoulder, the roads snaked
along to follow the floors of hollows, or shadowed
the course of creeks invisible through the dense
brush.

Only by the grace of a GPS program on his phone
was he able to find the switchback road that brought
him to the foot of the Cade driveway. Even with
that, he drove past the opening in the trees and had

to back up until he spied the metal mailbox covered in flaked paint. The name Cade was carved on the faces of the wooden support column by someone striving for neatness if not craft.

The trees grew right down the road to form an arbor overhead just beyond run-off ditches that ran along each narrow verge. He put the truck into reverse, leaning out the window to scan the trees along the opposite side of the road. Through the boles of poplars and scrub oak he could see the glimmer of sunlight coming down through branches just starting to bud with new leaves. Some oil drums with the lids cut away had been laid down in the ditch with a covering of gravel over them. He pulled the Ford over these and through the overgrowth that now covered what might have once been a driveway that led to a long-abandoned house or a cabin.

Inching along, he nosed the truck into the spot of sunlight. It was a clearing that provided just enough room to turn the truck around. He pointed the hood back the way he'd come to give him a clear view of the foot of the Cade driveway. He cut the engine and, without the heater running, could feel the cold begin to creep into the cab. He couldn't risk running the engine and giving himself away.

It was twenty degrees colder here than it was in Huntsville. The afternoon came sooner in these hollers than out on the flats. From a canvas bag he took out two Hot Spot pads and situated one under his rump. The other he pressed together in his gloved hands until he could feel the crystals inside activate and the warmth radiate from within. This one he stuck inside his coat against his stomach. With his ass and his belly warm, he undid the top of the one-liter thermos and poured himself a plastic cup of some Maxwell House fortified with Jim Beam.

He settled in for a long wait.

He thought over what he knew of this Levon Cade even though there wasn't much *to* know. Born in North Carolina but native to this county where he spent his whole life before joining the Marines straight out of high school. There was some indication of a sealed record with juvenile charges that Dollinger did not have access to. As a teenager, Cade did two short stretches at Neaves-Davis for offenses unknown.

His service record didn't reveal much of anything. He got married while still in the Corps and had a daughter. His wife Arlene died of some kind of cancer just after he was discharged. The only time he showed up on the radar after that was in court filings when he sued his in-laws for custody of Meredith Cade, his little girl. His mother-in-law was found murdered and father-in-law, a pediatrician, disappeared until he resurfaced a while back to face federal charges for running a pill mill in Florida.

Cade shows up in Alabama after a few years to live on his uncle's farm. Registers his little girl at the local public school along with another daughter named Hope who seemed to have popped up out of nowhere. The mystery deepens with an unemployed former Marine paying off all his uncle's back debts and the pair of them taking out a small business loan to go partners in a micro-distillery.

How any of that tied into this missing lawyer and Congressman Barnes was way outside Dollinger's ability to put together. For now. His plan was to follow this jarhead around awhile and see where it led him. He reasoned that Cade would not have brought the lawyer and the missing goodies home to his family. If he took Justin Hicks anywhere it was somewhere other than the Cade property.

Being a homegrown boy, Cade would know a million places back in these hills to stow away anything he wished to hide. Only a matter of time before he circled back to his hidey hole.

Two bacon and cheese sandwiches and a half thermos of coffee later, he saw a flicker of light through the trees on the opposite side of the road. He wiped at the windshield with the heel of his hand. Ice had rimed there in the hours he'd waited. It was full dark outside; the only light was the muted glow of a half-moon through a haze of clouds and the growing glare of the headlights coming down the driveway from the direction of the Cade place.

A truck poked its grill out onto the roadway. It was hard to tell what color it was other than it was a dark shade. The unique silhouette, as it turned right out of the drive, marked it as an Avalanche. The accent light above the rear plate made the numbers readable. It was the same truck that he saw on Bear's phone screen. Dollinger had also seen the front end clearly. The grill and bumper were unscarred. The headlight in place. The son of a bitch had the damage from the head-on repaired.

He gave the Avalanche some lead time before backing out of his hide and out onto the road surface. The red lights of the other truck disappeared out of sight around a curve. He knew from studying the area on Mapquest that the road that fronted the Cade property turned back onto the county road a few miles south of here. But that was only after almost twenty miles of loops and turns that followed the foot of the razorback ridgelines.

He could afford to hang back, only staying close enough to see the other truck's taillights now and then. That way he'd stay, near invisible, on Cade's ass the whole way out of the holler as the road followed a path as twisted as a hog's tail. He cinched up his seat harness as tight as he could and braced himself against the wheel. Still, his body swayed side to side on the washboard surface, once dropping a wheel into a pothole that made him strike the back of his head against the rear wall of the cab.

A few miles along the road he made a sharp turn around the brow of a granite promontory that jutted from the foot of the hillside. On the opposite side of the road the ground fell away to where a stream cut a rut along the base of the holler. The far end of the turn saw the roadway flatten out for a straight run along the creek bank for a mile or more.

The way ahead was dark. No taillights. No Avalanche.

Dollinger brought the Ford to a halt with a curse.

There was no way in hell the other truck got that far ahead of him. He was as close as could follow all the way down out of the holler. The other truck should have been no more than a hundred yards ahead as he came out onto the flat.

He spun the truck around in a three-point, the right tires dropping into the runoff ditch making the shocks scream and bouncing him clear off the seat cushion to strike his head on the ceiling of the cab. He gunned the Ford and it leapt out onto the broken asphalt to a juddering landing. From there he proceeded at a crawl, searching either side of the road for where the Avalanche had pulled off.

Three hairpin turns and a half mile back brought him to a 'Y' intersection he had not seen in passing before. The intersecting road veered off closer to the banks of the creek into the dark of the trees that grew there. He crept the Ford along down this rutted pathway, his head sticking from the open driver's side window despite the chill damp.

A few hundred yards down what was more a game trail than a navigable roadway he saw where tires had left the roadway. They cut through a hummock of dirt and into the shadows of the woods beyond a near invisible driveway opening. The deep passage of truck tires was clearly visible in the ochre mud.

Dollinger cut his lights but kept the Ford's engine turning. He stepped from the cab, boots squelching in the damp road surface. With a pocket flash held low, he examined the tire tracks. The muddy water in the treads had not settled yet.

This was where the son of a bitch had come to. Some godforsaken moonshiner's hideaway where no one would come looking. He held a hand cupped over the end of the flash and shone it along either side of the driveway opening. He was looking for a mailbox or some other marker of what might lay at the end of the dirt road that vanished into the gloom of the woods.

The light glanced off a stout wooden post. He led the beam up to the top where it was topped by a thick plank that ran over the opening of the driveway to another post to form an archway over the opening. Squinting upwards, he swept the light over the plank.

Carved into the wood were the initials W.C.A.

Beneath it, in smaller letters, the legend *Non Silba Sed Anthar*.

He sounded it out to himself as he read it, the words familiar. Dollinger searched his memory for the meaning.

"Not Self, But Others."

"God a'mighty." He breathed to himself before hurrying back to the F-150 to turn himself around for the trip back to 21st Century Alabama.

16

"Klan Klavern," Gage said, snickering.

"That's what the hell is it is, or was," Lew Dollinger said, his annoyance at his nephew growing. "Back in his time, your grandaddy was a kleagle in the Huntsville chapter."

"Kleagle, huh?" Gage simpered.

Bear, squeezed into the booth next to Gage, snorted bubbles into his Coke. They were at a Waffle House, a different one this time. Dollinger had them drive up the interstate to meet him outside Haley. Gage and Bear had come up in Bear's war machine. Now they were eating on his dime and laughing at him.

"Them old boys were a power in their day," Dollinger said. "Even more so in this part of the state. Had the governor on their side, and all. And here you're laughing like it's all a goddamn joke."

"You're the one saying all those silly-ass words," Gage said with an infuriating smile.

"Sounds like babytalk," Bear grinned, maple syrup running into his beard.

"It was code, I guess," Dollinger shrugged. "Like a secret way of talkin' to each other.

"And you found some kind of Klan hangout up here?" Gage asked.

"Well, it used to be anyways," Dollinger said. "I heard talk of Sugar Run back when I was a kid. Everyone in the state heard of the place. That's where real secret Klan shit happened. Big meetings, cross burnings, lynchings. There's even supposed to be a nigger cemetery back up there."

"This was all back then," Gage said.

"A place like that, where bad shit went down? That don't just fade away with time. Klan's smaller now but that only means it's all die-hards left, the real serious sumbitches."

"Gone underground," Gage nodded.

"And a place where nobody's ever going to go looking," Dollinger said and took a long sip of coffee.

"You followed this guy up there, the one you think he's the one took this lawyer. You think he's Klan?"

"Nothing in his records about that. But then, there wouldn't be, would there? Not if he was a real insider, one of the core members."

"You think the Klan had something to do with taking the lawyer?" Gage asked, nibbling a fry.

That was something that had occurred to Dollinger. In addition to advancing the interests of white supremacy, Jews and Catholics excluded, the night riders sometimes acted as vigilantes. In their past, they'd put on their hoods to settle scores, whipping or even hanging white men for rape, wife beating or theft.

The congressman was into some shady stuff that this lawyer was apparently privy to. Dollinger had no idea what Phillip Barnes's kink was, but he'd heard rumors that the man had a wild side. Maybe something he'd done had set the Klan on him. Hard to imagine it, looking at the frail old guy, that Barnes might howl naked at the moon or chase young tail. But then, no one knows the real heart of a man.

"I don't think so," Dollinger said. "I think it's more likely it's just a place no one would think to go snooping."

"And you need some help with your snooping," Gage said.

"I thought you boys could ride over there with me in that boat of Bear's. Ground's rough over that way."

"You mean ride with us," Gage corrected. "And what're you gonna pay for that ride? Or did you expect us to head back up in there to get our asses shot off as a personal favor to you?"

"I'll give you a hundred."

"Each."

"Each."

"And gas."

"And gas."

"A full tank."

Dollinger blew out a breath through his teeth and leaned forward to pull his wallet free.

"Can we get chocolate pie?" Bear asked in a small voice.

"Hon?" Gage said, waving a waitress over.

"He wants a slice of chocolate pie," Dollinger sighed.

"Half a pie," Gage said.

Bear beamed at the waitress, and she winced a smile back before turning for the pie case at the counter.

Dollinger counted out six fifties onto the tabletop. Gage scooped them up.

"All right," Gage said with a wink. "Soon's we're done with lunch we'll head on up to your Klan klagger."

"Klavern, you fucking moron," Dollinger snarled, dealing out a pair of twenties for the meal.

Bear covered his mouth to stem a spray of syrup.

17

"You have a friend," Merry said. It was more a pronouncement than a question.

"Who told you that?" Levon said.

"Uncle Fern. Said you have a friend might want to work at Blue Moon."

"I do and he might." Levon was setting a new post in one of the stalls inside the stable building. The old one had surrendered to dry rot, causing the hinges to be pulled from the wood by the weight of the slatted half-gate.

"He have a name? Do I know him?"

"Don't you have stalls to muck out?"

"Hopey's doing fine."

"I heard you say that," came Hope's voice from the stall across the aisle. She was forking through the hay and dumping clumps of manure into a barrow. The horse and pony were turned out in the paddock. The Abyssinian goat that Fern had named Tricky Dick lay atop a hay bale, watching them with his weird eyes.

"His name is Wesley. Wes," Levon said with a grunt as he raised the gate up to balance atop a pair of upended feed buckets. He set the gate in place and bent to get a pair of new brass hinges he bought at Home Depot that were still affixed to cardboard backs.

"He from around here?" Merry leaned a shoulder on the stall wall, making herself comfortable.

"He lives in county but he's from Tennessee originally."

"Why'd he move?"

"Likes the scenery, I guess."

"Was he in the Marines with you?"

"He was Army. We never met before."

"Where'd you meet him then?"

"Out hunting."

"When? The only time you've been hunting was that time with me back on Christmas break."

"That's when. He's the guy took a shot at us."

He ignored Merry's wide-eyed reaction as he set a hinge against the post to mark the spots with a pencil where he'd drill the pilot holes.

"And you're friends now?" Merry said when she'd recovered.

"What is happening?" Hope stepped from the stall she was mucking, alarmed at Merry's raised voice.

"Remember I told you about that man who shot at Daddy and me when we were hunting?" Merry pointed an accusing finger at Levon. "He made friends with the man!"

"It wasn't like that." Levon set the drill bit in the Hilti and chucked it in place. "I went up there to see who'd been shooting at us and why. All's he was doing was scaring us off."

Merry's bitter reply was cut off by the high whirr of the drill as Levon bored the pilot holes.

"He's been living up there on his own." Levon unchucked the bit to replace it with a Phillips head screw tip. "I talked to him. Decided to help him out a little, is all."

"Living in the woods?" Merry's expression softened. "He was in the war?"

"Yeah. Iraq for a couple of deployments. Had to get away."

"Is he still living in the woods?"

"I found him another place. A few hollers west of here."

"And he wants to go to work for Uncle Fern?"

"Well, I thought I'd drive over there later today to talk to him about it. Break it slow."

"What's he know about distilling?"

"What do *you* know about it, Merryberry?"

"Can I meet him?"

"If I can talk him into taking the job, you'll see him all the time." Levon interrupted her next question with the sound of the drill sinking screws home to secure the first brass hinge plate in place.

"I mean, meet him today," she said when he'd secured the last screw home. "Drive over there with you."

Levon turned to meet her eyes.

"What are you thinking?" she asked, eyes slits.

"Thinking of reasons I can't take you with me," he said, turning back to the gate to shift it into place within the frame.

"Well, I'm going!" Another Merry Cade pronouncement.

"Me too!" Hope called from the next stall.

Levon sighed and returned to setting the new gate between the posts.

18

Wesley was seated on the two-holer inside the outhouse, reading a *Playboy* interview with Miles Davis in the muted light of the sun coming through the translucent plexi ceiling.

He heard the sound of a truck approaching and rose to greet Levon's return. The motor grew louder, the vehicle racing closer. It came to a stop that sprayed gravel that rattled against the doublewide's siding.

Something in the sounds put a hitch in his step as he buckled his jeans. He stopped to look through a gap in the boards before stepping from the outhouse. A truck he'd never seen before. A GMC all jacked up on fat knobby tires. A crew cab with a short bed painted in forest camo trimmed in black. A real hoopie war machine. Three men were climbing out of it. All white dudes, and all armed. Two shotguns and a tricked-out AR-15 with all the bells and whistles.

This was turning into a wrong place-wrong time situation. Nobody who'd be showing up in a place like this in a truck like that would mean Wesley any good. No good at all.

One of them was the whitest white man Wesley had ever seen. Tall dude with fish belly white complexion approached the door of the doublewide with a pump gun raised. A big linebacker-looking redneck with another shotty was covering the door for him. A third guy, the one with the semi-auto, was sighting down his barrel to scan the acreage.

"No one here," AR-15 said.

"You don't know that," the really, really white guy said, holding open the screen door to allow the bigger guy to shoulder check the entry door. It swung inward with a crash. Stupid assholes. He'd left it unlocked but they hadn't even tried the knob.

"'Less they walked here," AR-15 said. "No car. No truck."

"Anyone inside?" Whitey called. An answer from inside the doublewide Wesley couldn't make out.

"See? Nobody's home," AR-15 said.

"Even better. We search for the goods and set-up an ambush," Whitey said.

"What if the stuff you're lookin' for ain't here?"

"Then we get this fella to *tell* us where it is." Whitey spoke as though to a small child. "Now pull that truck outta sight somewhere and come inside."

"Gotta use the shitter first, cuz," AR-15 said. "Just about lost my mud comin' up that last ten mile of road."

"Spare me," Whitey said and vanished inside the doublewide with the linebacker.

AR-15, his rifle shoulder-slung now, walked for the outhouse, undoing his jeans as he ambled closer.

Wesley waited, a shoulder pressed to the inside

of the door, the pull handle in his fist. He sighted through a narrow gap in the planks as the man stepped closer, intent on undoing his belt. When the shadow of the man filled the slit between the boards, Wesley threw his weight hard against the door.

The edge of the heavy planks took the guy square in the face, spilling him backwards onto his ass. Wesley leapt from the outhouse to bend over the man, trying to free the sling of the rifle where it was tangled under the man's back. The guy was bleeding from where he'd taken the door edge full in the nose, blood pouring from a gash across the bridge. Dazed but not unconscious, the guy was putting up a feeble struggle while gagging on swallowed blood. One hand gripped the web strap of the rifle.

The screen door banged, and Wesley looked up to see Whitey on the stoop, pig eyes gone wide over the barrel of the shotgun coming up in his fists.

"Bear!" he called out and let loose a snapshot charge of buck that missed Wesley to ventilate the outhouse.

Wesley weighed his choices in a heartbeat. Get that rifle freed. Make for the truck. Or make for the woods.

The rifle was not coming loose. The fallen man had a white-knuckle grip on the sling now. He was blinking away the blood in his eyes to stare with a mad rage at Wesley.

There was no assurance the keys were still in the truck's ignition.

He was up on his feet and around the side of the outhouse, intent on keeping it between him and the doublewide as he sprinted for the trees. A second charge of buck tore the roof off the shitter. The corrugated plexi sheet spinning away on a spray of glittering splinters. Voices called out behind him, bellowing names and curses.

Wesley kept his eyes on the shadows under the pines in a dead run. They'd move around the outhouse to put him in their line of sight. Another fifty yards and he'd be out of the lethal effective range of the shotguns. The guy with the rifle would be out of the fight long enough for Wesley to make the woods.

He hoped. He prayed. He ran like hell.

The pump guns boomed in near tandem behind him, both men firing wild. Shot whistled past taking the tops off milkweed ahead of him. Another round boomed. Something punched him in the shoulder. The impact nearly caused him to stumble. His right arm went numb. He could feel a warm wetness on his back. He'd caught a ball or three of shot. Fuck that shit. He ran on, coming to a slight dip in the ground that would take him out of sight of his pursuers.

Concealed from view for a few seconds, he cut sharply left to come up the other side of the dip a dozen paces away from his former trajectory. Voices raised far behind him, talking over one another. They were closer, chasing on foot. They hadn't used the truck, or they'd already be on him. Thank Jesus for small blessings.

He brushed through a sagging clump of sumacs to duck under a lowering pine bough. Shot screamed past above him sending needles to rain down as he ran. He was in the gloom of the trees now, the branches and boles of the dense growth cutting him off from the view of his pursuers. He changed course, running to the left just inside the shelter of the trees.

Run or hide. There were only three of them. If he could throw them off long enough, he could slip outside their search path. Elude them long enough and they'd tire of looking for him. That still left them free to do what they came here to do.

He'd heard enough of their conversation to know they'd come here for Levon. It had to have something to do with the man they'd buried. The baby-raping lawyer whose body was resting under the sand of the playground out front of the doublewide.

Probably even more to do with the shitpile of the lawyer's papers, hard drives and cash money Levon showed up with back around the start of the year.

Wesley's mind raced over his options. He couldn't just run off. He couldn't leave Levon to these fuckers. And he was too far from anywhere to go for help. And bringing the law up in here would only make for a whole different set of problems.

He moved, slower now, more cautious, as to make less noise. The men were calling to one another. All three now somewhere behind him. Calls and responses as they worked out a search plan. Their voices echoing in the trees. They were in the woods with him. Two of them anyway.

Blood was running out from the sleeve of his coat. He tucked his right hand inside his shirt to stop it dripping so as not to leave a trail. They hadn't picked up any sign; they were still moving further into the woods, veering away from his path along the rim of the trees. He'd work his way north as far as he could, until he was beyond the risks of immediate detection. It would be dark in a few hours.

The numbness in his arm was receding to be

replaced by an electric tingle. The pain would come soon. Nothing to be done about that. The bleeding was a more pressing issue. He'd need to deal with that and soon.

The temperature would drop with the sun going down. That would slow the blood loss. He'd only worn a light coat over his flannel shirt to go out to the outhouse. Exposure would be a problem. He might survive a night out in this, but the effect would be crippling. Between the killing cold and the loss of blood, he'd be out of the fight by morning.

He'd be no good to Levon or himself then.

Wesley crouched behind the thick trunk of an elder. He sucked in a breath and held it in to listen hard to the sounds around him. The three men were well back of him, cursing and calling. He'd stay where he was, listening for his opening to change position.

He wasn't going to run any more. After a few months spent walking Sugar Run, he knew the ground. Not like it was home, but he knew it way better than these fuckers did. He had a strong sense these three had never been up this holler before.

Two of them were moving deeper into the woods, following the former line of his retreat, to take them away from where he crouched. He listened hard, eyes shut and ears straining. One of them was hanging back by the doublewide while the other two walked on up the wooded incline. He heard his voice calling instructions, the answers from the other two growing fainter with distance.

It was Wesley's guess it was Whitey McWhiteman standing ground while the other two played hounds. He was the boss of the trio. His attitude and the way he gave orders made that clear. And he was dressed better than them in hick *chic* like a Grand Ol' Opry star in his snakeskin boots and leather coat. Even his shotgun was uptown.

The pair climbing through the trees were calling back, voices dimmer. The thwack and crunch of them passing through the trees faded to nothing as the separation increased. Whitey's voice rasped in anger. They were bitching and he was telling them tough shit in reply.

Wesley crouched, shoulder aching dully now. He'd give it a count of one hundred before moving back the way he came. He was all out of options. There was only one way forward for him. If he could thread the needle between Whitey and his boys, he might have a chance.

If not, he guessed he wouldn't be the first brother to wind up in a shallow grave up in here.

19

The cinder block shed, its metal roof spotted green with moss, sat hidden among the trees. It was built into the natural slope of the hillside to keep its contents cool.

Wesley fought down a feeling of vertigo as he moved at a crouch toward the sagging steel door that leaned in the frame at the front of the shed. With his left hand he eased the door open, wincing at the squeal from the remaining hinge. It was encrusted with rust from years of neglect, and he regretted not oiling it. To him, it sounded as loud as a fire siren in the woods made silent by the explosion of shotguns.

He squinted through the gloom at the inventory that rested on the shelves of the shed. Wooden crates marked Redstone Arsenal. Steel ammo boxes marked the same with stamps from the Army Corps of Engineers. The crates contained #3 dynamite that God alone knew the stability of after being stored here for decades. The ammo boxes held det cord, pencil fuses and other tools of the trade that he had grown familiar with over his time in the

Army. Explosives were part of his MOS with the 8th Cavalry. Blowing holes in walls back in Fallujah and Tikrit.

Leaning back against the damp wall of the shed, he searched his mind for a better option than the one he was considering. The cloying dizziness he felt, probably from blood loss, wasn't helping his thought process. An instructor at Bragg once told him, "Even a bad plan is better than no plan at all." So, even this rank shittiest of all shitty plans was better than either bleeding out in the woods or letting these fuckers find him. And he'd need to act fast as he could feel his levels of strength and concentration failing.

Wesley held a rusted ammo box clamped between his knees and undid the latch. He dumped the contents on the floor and sorted through it for the gear he'd need.

***

Lew Dollinger stood at the rim of the acre of mown grass that ringed the doublewide and peered into the tree line for signs of movement.

He cursed himself for not handing his cousin Gage and that mountain of stupid walkie-talkies before they took off running after the coon. He had a pair he'd brought along in the truck and a heap of good they were doing sitting there. He checked his cell and there were zero bars and a polite "No Available Network" on the screen. Deep in this hillbilly holler he couldn't even reach Gage by phone.

Hands cupped either side of his mouth he called out to the pair moving somewhere out of sight under the trees along the slope.

"You see anything?" he shouted.

The answer that echoed down the slope was unintelligible.

"I want that coon alive now!" His voice grew hoarse as he strained to reach them.

One of them called back, the sound little more than a murmur.

He'd just have to hope Gage and Bear could run the nigger down before dark. He didn't give himself good odds on that happening. They'd come back after a while either pushing their quarry ahead of them or empty-handed. A fresh set of decisions would wait till then.

What in the name of sweet Christ was a nigger doing hiding in the shithouse on Klan property anyway? That had to be about the last thing Dollinger would have expected coming up here. The black man had to be squatting, was the only thing he could imagine. And it was clear from the condition of the grounds and the buildings that this had long ago ceased to be a center of Klan activity in this county. Which brought into question what business this Levon Cade had up in Sugar Run. Maybe the nigger was a friend of his. All the more reason to catch the nigger, alive hopefully.

Sumacs grew thick around the roofs of derelict vehicles gone orange with corrosion. He pushed fresh shells into his shotgun as he watched the fronds of the long spindly stalks for any movement. Tempting as it was to return to the interior of the doublewide to resume his search, Dollinger kept watch on the trees and brush to the west.

What made most sense was that this was some kind of hidey-hole for Cade. Best bet was, after he'd grabbed Hicks down in Huntsville, he brought the lawyer up here to hold him. There was no ransom demand of any kind, so it wasn't a kidnapping. If the congressman was right, the lawyer had a sizable amount of cash on him when he was abducted. Also, a collection of damning evidence that his employer wanted back really bad. Most probably, that evidence was potentially worth more than the cash money. That piqued Dollinger's interest. He knew Phil Barnes was into some shady doings, that was the rumor anyhow. Could be Dollinger might just go into business for himself once he found it. Retire from being the congressman's coonhound with one fat payoff. The thought of it frayed at the edges of his patience.

"You found that nigger yet, Gage?" His voice was a high keening shriek now, his pale face beet red with the effort.

No reply.

The tops of one of the sumacs nearest him shimmied. It was alone in its movement. It wasn't the wind.

He raised the shotgun to his shoulder to train it on the suspect motion. There was a clink, a metallic sound from somewhere in the brush. Over the tops of the sumacs a box sailed in his direction. The dark green box turned end over end to come to a landing out of sight in the tall grass a hundred feet or so from where he stood.

Dollinger fired a load of buck toward where he'd seen the sumacs rustle. He drew back the pump for another shot. Before he could depress the trigger, a dull roar filled his ears and the world before him vanished in a rising wave of red earth.

The concussive wave of the blast lifted him clean

off his feet to land him hard on his ass. His skull felt like it was trapped in the sudden painful grip of a vise. The pump gun flew from his hands to land out of reach. He rose, back aching, to his knees as a haze of dust washed over him and clods of earth rained down all around. On hands and knees, he crawled, blinded by the stinging fog of particulates, toward where he thought the truck was parked. Gasping and choking he somehow bumped against one of the fat tires of Bear's truck. He clawed himself to his feet and found the door handle.

***

Wesley dropped to the ground after tossing the ammo can overhand toward the whiter-than-white dude standing in the open on the other side of the brush. He pressed his hands to his ears and opened his mouth wide. He was weak now and throwing southpaw. The can, and its contents of a block of C-4 primed with a pencil fuse, failed to get within killing range of the albino motherfucker.

When the roar died down, he rose to his feet. The white dude, dusted pink now with pulverized Alabama clay, had reached the truck and was climbing inside. Wesley fought down the pain radiating from his torn shoulder to swing back a second ammo can and fling it in an arc toward the truck. It went off a foot shy of the ground. Jagged metal shards shredded white hot from the ammo can whistled just inches above where he lay prone on the ground. He raised himself up to look through the chemical stink that remained after the explosion.

The redneck war wagon was making a wide turn before the doublewide. The tailgate and right quarter panel were peppered with holes from the second, closer, blast. The truck took off south, raising twin rooster tails of dirt as it bounced and bucked over the rough ground in search of the rutted drive that led back to the road.

Wesley stumbled from the brush, ears ringing. He found the white dude's shotgun, a Benelli, lying in the grass. He hefted it and, one handed, sent an already chambered round of buck after the fleeing truck. More as a senseless act of defiance than anything else. His right arm useless and unable to pump in a fresh cartridge, he tossed the gun aside to seek the shelter of the outhouse. He reached the far side of the little cinder block shack just as the timed charge he set under an abandoned John Deere went off with a thunderclap that shook the ground under his feet. Two blocks of C-4 this time. A tall plume of dust, vegetation and tractor parts raised by four sticks of dynamite blocked out the light of the setting sun.

20

"You hear that?" Bear said, turning on the trail to look back to where a dome shaped cloud of dust was dropping back to the ground.

"Shit," Gage seethed. "They heard that in Birmingham."

"My truck," Bear said with a low moan and started back down the way they'd come.

The deep thud of the second blast stopped him in his tracks. He turned back to Gage with a stricken look. A look of confusion, like a child lost at the state fair. Gage looked down through the trees to see that the second eruption raised a drifting tower of white smoke that mixed with the crimson fog of the prior detonation.

The third blast startled them both as the sloping trail under them turned to the deck of a ship at sea. Bear fell hard against a birch bole. Gage stumbled backward to land flat on his back. The floor of the holler below them was invisible now in a rising cloud of hot dust. The sound of a shotgun discharging reached them through the rumbling echoes of the most recent explosion still rebounding off the walls of the holler.

Bear stared into the thick wall of smoke rising through the trees toward them.

"What do we do, Gage?" he said in a quavering voice that matched his little boy lost expression.

"Run like hell," Gage said and turned to do just that.

***

"You hear that?" Merry said, turned to peer into the trees racing by.

"It is thunder?" Hope said where she sat between Levon and Merry on the front seat of the Avalanche.

"Not a cloud in the sky," Levon said, leaning forward to look up the slender portion of the late afternoon sky he could see through the pine tops.

"There's another one," Merry said. A report, a sharper one this time, followed by a low boom, came from somewhere off to their left.

Hope pressed closer to Levon. He took a hand from the wheel to place it on her knee.

"Sounds like blasting. Maybe someone's clearing stumps," Levon said. He made a hard left to turn off the township road to follow the switchback that ran along the creekbank at the base of Sugar Run.

A third peal, louder than the others, died away to a growling sound that went on and on like a warning from an angry beast. It was from somewhere north of the road they were on.

"That one was closer," Merry said.

Hope was clutching Levon's right arm now.

"More like we're getting closer to it." Levon considered pulling to the side of the road at the next place where the shoulder would allow.

They were coming to a tight turn to the right when a big pickup raised high on broad-tread tires fishtailed out of the curve toward them. Levon jerked the wheel right into reeds growing along the boggy verge of the single lane road. There was just enough passage for the truck to tear past them. The monster tires pelted the Avalanche with aggregate and clots of mud as it continued on without slowing to disappear around a turn.

"You girls all right?" Levon said, inching the truck out of the muck and back onto the gravel surface.

"He never even tapped the brakes!" Merry said, out of her seat straps now and kneeling on the seat to look back through the rear window of the cab.

"You okay, Hopey?"

Hope nodded, smiling up at him, eyes wide with alarm behind the lenses of her glasses.

Levon drove them toward the curve ahead. The hairs on the back of his neck stood up. His grip on the wheel tightened. His eyes scanned the woods that closed in on the left and right sides of the roadway.

"I want you girls to unbuckle and lay on the floor behind me."

Merry helped Hope out of her belt and dropped the middle console down so they could both clamber into the backseat.

There were deep tracks gouged out of the dirt at the overgrown opening to the drive up to the compound. Broad tracks that left swaths of clumped soil behind where the truck that passed them broke out of the woods. Levon rolled down his window as he pulled off the roadway into the trees. There was a sharp metallic smell in the air along with the scent of rotten eggs. The slanted sunlight coming through the woods either side of the narrow trail was muted by a spreading haze of fine dust. It powdered the hood of the Avalanche.

It was quiet now, but someone had detonated some serious ordnance up at the compound. He thought about turning around as soon as he had enough clearance. He thought about maybe even trying to catch up to the guy who was in such a hurry to get out of here. Only that guy would be miles from here by now, gone up any number of roads that branched away to all points over the northern end of the county. And those explosions would mean that Wesley had run into serious problems or was blasting some caps to discourage unwanted visitors.

Once clear of the trees, Levon punched the gas along the drive. He slowed when the roofs of the doublewide and picnic portico came in view. He approached the buildings slowly, trying to see through the spreading smoke to see if there were any other strange vehicles around. He saw no movement of any kind and braked the Avalanche to a stop in the clearing before the buildings.

"Daddy," Merry said from the back seat. "There's someone moving over there."

"Where?" Levon opened his door and stepped from the cab. With the same motion he drew the .45 auto he kept holstered at the small of his back.

"By that shack," Merry said.

Levon blinked through the acrid smoke as he neared the outhouse, Colt held in a two-handed grip. He swept left and right before moving closer. He stepped over fresh ruts in the soil caused by the fleeing truck.

It was Wesley.

He was seated on the ground, his back against the outhouse wall. One side of his shirt was black with drying blood all down one sleeve. He looked up at Levon with a weak smile.

"Hey, Levon," he said, mumbling.

"Are there more of them?" Levon. He holstered the Colt and dropped to a knee.

"They run off." Wesley's eyelids fluttered.

"How many?"

"Two. 'Nother one took off in a truck."

"Stay with me."

"I'm just tired is all. There was two more."

"Where are they now?" Levon pulled the man forward a bit to look at the wounds in his shoulder.

"Took off somewhere. They was on the hill to the west side of the holler."

"Okay. That's good. We're gonna get you some help, okay?" Levon turned to call back to the truck. Merry was already running to him, Hope close behind. Merry had the toolbox that contained his first aid supplies in her hand.

"Wesley, these are my daughters," Levon said as he began cutting away the bloody shirt with his clasp knife. "Merry and Hope. Girls, this is Wesley Ruskin."

"Hey, girls," Wesley made a feeble attempt at a grin.

"Looks like you caught two rounds. No exit wounds." Levon dabbed away the blood from two swollen holes in Wesley's shoulder.

"It's buckshot," Wesley said, taking a breath through his teeth as the gauze touched the wounds.

"Shit!" he said, letting the breath out before

turning eyes to Merry and Hope. "Sorry, ladies."

"They've heard worse," Levon said, taking a pair of syringes from a plastic packet. "I'm gonna stop the bleeding. But if you're gonna be a little bitch, I'll give you a shot first."

"It does sting," Wesley nodded, eyes pressed shut.

A shot of lidocaine near the wound site followed by two milligrams of morphine in Wesley's right arm.

"Run and get me a bottle of water from the truck, Hope," Levon said. The girl raced back toward the open rear door of the Avalanche.

"What do you need me to do, Daddy?" Merry asked.

"Tear open some of those gauze packs and stand by," Levon said, unloading a dropper of Mercurochrome into a bottle of alcohol. "This is gonna burn, bro."

Wesley just nodded.

Levon sprayed the wound area with the mix and wiped away as much blood as he could before applying a thick pad of gauze that he tied in place across the man's chest.

"Gonna have to make it tight."

"Go on ahead. I feel that second shot kicking in." Wesley offered him a sloppy grin, eyelids at half-mast.

"Tell me about these men."

"Two went up the hill. One was a bigass wrestler type. The other some skinnyass redneck."

"The one in the truck?"

"He was in charge. Whitest motherfucker I've ever seen. Like he'd been dipped in bleach." Wesley pressed his lips tight. Levon applied more pressure to the wounds.

Levon cinched the bandage tight. Wesley grunted despite the embrace of the painkillers. Levon secured the dressing in place with strips of surgical tape torn off a roll by Merry. Hope knelt by the wounded man and helped him take a few sips from a gallon jug. Levon rested back on one leg and examined the bandage. There was no sign of blood coming through. It would do for now, until he could get those slugs out. Wesley looked dreamily at them all.

"Merryberry, I need you to do something now," Levon said. "And you can say no if you think it's the wrong thing to do or maybe you're just too scared."

"Just tell me what to do," Merry said.

"Do you think you could take Wesley to Jessie's?"

"You mean drive the truck?"

"You drive the tractor on the farm no problem. And I know Fern's let you drive his Ford a few times."

"As long as you trust me to do it."

"Wouldn't ask if I didn't think you were up to it. Just go back out the way we came. Go right to Jessie's. As soon as you get where you can call ahead you call her and tell her I'm asking for a favor, the same kind of favor she did for my cousin Teddy. That way she'll be ready when you get there."

"What do I do?" Hope asked. She was holding Wesley's hands, eyes fixed in his face.

"You go along with your sister. You play nurse while Merry drives."

"Where will you be?" Hope asked, turned her gaze to him.

"He'll be hunting," Merry said.

21

Men, like animals, follow the path of least resistance when fleeing. On flat ground they'll move in an unconscious circle back the way they came. In hilly country, they'll move downhill every time.

Levon trotted at double time just inside the tree line. There was no need for quiet for now. The men he was after would be well out of earshot by now. Probably suffering some hearing loss from the multiple explosions. Certainly confused. They'd head away from danger, heading deeper into the holler, following the natural funnel formed by the steep slopes to the east and west.

The screen of pines would shield him from view but allow him sight of the open valley floor. Eventually, the two men he was after would break into the open. They'd have to once they realized that the base of the holler ended in a high, rocky bluff.

A few miles along, as he neared the crotch of the V-shaped depression, Levon slowed his pace. He stopped to listen. He could hear voices ahead. He couldn't pick out words. An exchange. Hard to pin down its source as the voices rebounded through the trees. He moved further at an easy pace, eyes scanning the green shadows ahead, ears attuned to the direction of the men's conversation.

He broke from cover, his modified M4 raised to his shoulder. Two men, one a huge bear of a man and the other smaller, were down on a bank of the creek. It was Sugar Run, the rivulet that gave the holler its name. Knee deep at most and choked with cattails.

The large man was standing, a pump shotgun in his fists. The smaller was seated on the ground in the process of pulling off his socks. A pair of work boots and a customized AR-15 lay on the grass by him. They'd been arguing as Levon approached. One saying that they needed to cross the creek. The other complaining that the water would be ice cold. The first calling him a little bitch and to start taking his boots off.

Levon hoped to surprise them while they were removing their shoes. The big man was still reluctant to get his feet wet. Levon fired three rounds into him center mass.

The heavy Beowulf slugs sent the big man stumbling back into the cattails where he lost his footing and fell with a splash of mud. The smaller man sat frozen.

"Hands where I can see them," Levon said, his sights on the seated man as he moved closer.

The seated man raised his hands, a white sock dangling from his fingers. Levon put two more slugs into the big man lying face down in the reeds. He swung sights back on the seated man.

"On your belly," Levon moved in, putting a foot on the AR. "Hands on the back of your head. Fingers twined."

The man did as he was told. Levon planted a knee in his back and patted him down. A Glock in his waistband. A clasp knife with a curved blade on his belt. Levon tossed both out into the creek. He rose and picked up the AR which he slung over one shoulder.

"Sit up."

The man scrabbled awkwardly to rest his ass in the mud. He eyed Levon with a look of what he probably hoped resembled defiance. Eyes wide and nose wrinkled. It came off as false bravado masking fear.

"Hands at the back of your head."

The man complied, moving his gaze from Levon's face to the barrel end of the M4.

"What are you doing here?" Levon asked.

"We just come up here to hunt. Heard there was a fat herd of white tail up this way."

"This late in the day?"

"You know. We were gonna do some jacklighting." Hunting by searchlight.

"Bullshit. Where's your lamp?"

"Dropped it a ways back."

"More bullshit. Are you Klan?"

The man's façade of boldness vanished in an expression of honest surprise.

"You mean KKK? No fucking way," the man said, shaking his head.

"Then what brings you here? And why'd you shoot my friend?"

"The nig—your friend attacked us first. Had hand grenades and shit like that."

"You start telling me the truth or end up like your

buddy there."

The seated man turned to look at his companion lying still in the cattails. He swallowed hard, eyes darting. He was making an appraisal of his options. Levon had seen the look many times before. The man's bare toes clutched at the mud in an unconscious gesture that told Levon he was considering flight.

"Don't be stupid," Levon said, voice easier now, offering brotherly advice.

"You're gonna kill me." The man's voice was almost child-like, quavering and rising an octave.

"Not if you tell me what I need to hear," Levon lied.

***

"I'm sorry," Wesley said from the back seat where he was strapped in, sitting up. Hope was with him, offering him sips of water.

"It's okay," Merry assured him as she drove. "Blood washes right off those seat covers."

"Not that."

His voice was weak, drowsy. Blood loss and the effects of the shot. Merry wanted to keep him talking.

"Then what are you sorry for?"

"I shot at you. You and your dad."

"Yeah. He told me about that."

"Levon told you that was me?"

"Daddy doesn't keep things from me. He used to and it never worked out so well."

"I only meant to scare you," Wesley said.

"Well, you sure did that!" she said but not in a mean way.

"Still a real dick move. Sorry."

"You just gonna apologize the whole way?"

Merry was working to keep him talking, keep him awake. She sat forward, leaning over the wheel to keep the ride smooth as she could manage. It was getting dark out. Her focus was fixed on the narrow tunnel created by the headlights. This stretch of road was never in that good a shape at the best of times. Now, after a season of snow and ice, its surface was holed and rutted and wash-boarded more than usual. She was balancing caution with speed to get to Jessie's place before her passenger died.

She came off the goat path switchback onto a county road and the ride evened out. Merry pressed down the gas.

"Hope, check the bars," she said.

"We have two," Hope said.

Merry spared a glance at the rearview to see her adopted sister looking at the screen of her phone. Hope was holding up fine after her initial surprise. The little girl was making sure their father's friend stayed hydrated. She volunteered to ride in the back with the man. Merry realized that she shouldn't be surprised. Hope told her some of what she experienced in the weeks long trip from Guatemala to the US Border. Merry knew there were things Hope had seen and heard that she did not want to talk about. God alone knew what the little girl had gone through. No wonder something like helping a gunshot stranger didn't faze her all that much.

"Call Jessie and put her on speaker phone," Merry said, giving the Avalanche a punch along a straight section.

22

It was practically a minor miracle, but Lew Dollinger found his way out of the maze of single and two-lane roads to find a north/south pike that would take him back to the main highway. He breathed easier when he saw his first sign for state road 231. He relaxed his grip, fingers tingling and numb from the death's grip he'd maintained on the wheel since his escape from Sugar Run.

He thought, but only for a moment or two, about turning around. His cousin and Bear were still back there. They were up the hill in the trees and well clear of the sticks of TNT or whatever it was that crazy nigger was throwing. Those boys were no strangers to the woods. They'd know how to get themselves clear. He considered pulling over and checking a map, maybe finding whatever road that might run behind the foot of the holler. He could wait there until the boys crossed it.

Scratch that, he thought as he pulled onto the southbound route of the state road. His instinct was to put distance between him and whoever tried to blow his ass to kingdom come. No way he was driving back into that clusterfuck, especially in the dark. By now, the dynamite flinging coon might have whistled up a small army to beat the bushes for Gage and Bear. Dollinger was not about to get into that sticky a mess.

Besides, once they were in the clear they could call him. He'd swing back this way tomorrow when it was daylight and pick them up. Maybe he'd pull into the next Quality Inn and take a room to await their call. He patted the pockets of his coat looking for his phone. It was gone. Probably lost it when that blast knocked him on his ass. He lost his Benelli too. Thousand-dollar shotgun and now that goddamn crazy nigger had it.

If Gage called him, it would be at home on his landline. He'd drive home, take a shower, and watch some ball until his cousin called him. Get a good night's sleep and drive back up here to pick the boys up. Then tell Phil Barnes all he found was a dry hole. The congressmen wasn't paying near enough for him to be poking his nose into Klan hideouts and facing down bomb-throwing brothers.

Dollinger felt bad about leaving Gage and Bear behind. But then, it was only for tonight. And he'd done a lot of things he'd regretted in his life and not a one of them had killed him.

Regrets gave way to hunger. He drove south, checking out the exit signs to look for the next Waffle House.

***

It was full dark by the time Gage finished telling all he knew to the stranger holding a rifle on him. It was getting cold. His ass was numb from sitting on the damp ground. His bare feet were turning blue. His shoulders were on fire from holding his fingers interlaced against the back of his head.

"This cousin of yours, was he a cop once?" the stranger asked.

"He was a sheriff's deputy down Perry County. Only that was years ago when I was a kid."

"So, what is he now?"

"I dunno. He does things for folks. For cash money."

"Like a private detective?"

"Like Magnum? Like that?"

"Something like that. What kind of folks does he help?"

"Lawyers, maybe? Folks who have money. Lew's always got a dog-chokin' roll of cash on him."

"He tell you who he's working for now?"

"Never said. Somebody with deep pockets."

"What'd you come up here looking for?"

"Some fella that Lew was lookin' for. A lawyer from Huntsville. We were lookin' for him and some stuff might be with him."

"Stuff?"

"Papers and files and shit like that."

The stranger stood silent, his face in a shadow. In the absence of further questions, Gage asked his own.

"You a Klansman, mister?"

"Why'd you ask that?"

"Lew said this was a Klan hangout, this whole holler. Told us all kinds of secret shit happened up in here."

The stranger said nothing.

"'Cause I got no problem with the Klan, okay?"

Gage said. "And I can keep a secret. Do it all the time. I'm no big fan of niggers. Jews neither. Might have even joined you guys."

Gage wished he could see the stranger's face to determine if any of his guff was having an impact. He continued to make his case.

"I think I mighta killed that nigger back there. I know I winged him. If you want, you and me can go lookin'. Maybe find him and finish him off if he ain't dead already."

"Put your boots on."

"Yes, sir?" Gage said.

He reached for his boots, his shoulders stiff from holding his arms raised so long. Still seated, he stretched out a hand for the boots. There was a flash of light and, as hard as he reached, the boots seemed further and further from his fingertips. A second flash and none of it mattered any more.

Levon slung the M4 back on his shoulder by the dead man's AR already hung there. He crouched over the smaller of the two men and rifled through pockets, removing a ring of keys, a cell phone, wallet and a billfold. He did the same for the fat one, stripping him of wallet, cash, cell phone, a can of Skoal and a few stray shotgun rounds. He pocketed the phones to destroy later. The rest, wallets, cash and keys, he stowed in one of the dead man's boots.

No one would come looking for either of these men. At least not any law. This Dollinger they were both working for might come back. If he did, he'd be armed for war and have company. More likely, from Levon's point of view and experience, Dollinger would have already cut his losses. There was little possibility the people Dollinger worked for would want him to involve the law. There was way too much to hide. Though they might use other means.

Whatever the upshot of today's events, Levon confirmed that the lawyer Hicks had a master. And that master knew all about Levon Cade and where to find him. The best course now was to leave the two men by the creek to the foxes and coyotes. That would leave less to bury if he ever got back up this way.

He had greater concerns now. Like making sure his family was safe.

Levon transferred the contents of the boot to the pockets of his barn coat and followed the creek back toward the compound.

23

"I hope your father doesn't plan on making a habit of this," Jessie said as she finished administering a follow up shot of morphine into an IV line she'd run into Wesley's arm. He sat stripped to the waist atop an examination table.

"Sorry," Merry said.

"Sorry," Wesley said, voice slurred.

"I need you to sit up and stay awake," Jessie said to her patient as she injected more lidocaine into three places around the pair of wounds. "Do not go into shock on me."

"Yes, ma'am." Wesley said, a little too loud.

"He's lost a lot of blood." Jessie washed the wound, spraying it from a bottle of distilled water. "It's the one thing I don't have. Human blood. And he'll lose more when I take out these slugs."

"He's type O," Merry said. She'd turned over Wesley's arm. His blood type was tattooed on the inside of his right wrist just below an Army eagle. "I'm the same type. So's my daddy."

"I'll run a line, okay?" Jessie pulled open a drawer to remove a sealed plastic pouch containing a new trocar and IV line. "But we'd better hope Levon shows up before long."

Merry took a seat next to Wesley and bared her arm for Jessie to wipe it clean with an alcohol swab.

"Sorry," Wesley murmured, fighting to keep his eyes open.

"He apologizes a lot," Merry said, making a fist.

"Unlike some guy we know," Jessie said seeking a vein on Merry's arm. "Big pinch."

***

"The old Boy Scout camp?" Fern said once he got the dogs quieted down.

"The one off the creek road." Levon sounded hoarse on the phone.

"I know where it is. What the hell you doing up there, and why do you sound out of breath?"

"'Cause I climbed up here out of Sugar Run to get a signal."

"Sugar Run? And what the hell were you doing *there?*"

"I'll tell you on the ride back. I need you to come get me."

"Your truck break down?"

"No, Merry took it to Jessie's."

"Merry? What the—"

"Just come get me, old man. We've got shit to do." Levon broke the connection.

"Who wants to go for a ride?" Fern said to the dogs who rushed to the kitchen door, nails clicking on the tile floor.

***

Wesley was resting in a painkiller haze in a leather recliner in the Hamer family room. Jessie had removed the pair of single-aught lead balls from

LEVON'S PREY | 119

the muscle tissue in his shoulder. The harder work was making sure all the debris the lead had carried with it was cleaned from the wounds. Flecks of cloth from his shirt and the germs and bacteria that were probably present on them could still cause a massive infection. She shot him full of antibiotics to help him combat that potential after suturing him up and applying clean bandages. He was comfortable now and sedated, covered in blankets and a banana bag IV drip to re-hydrate him.

"Pressure and pulse are okay. But I still don't like his color," Jessie said, taking Wesley's pulse.

"I can give more blood," Merry offered.

"Not another drop from you, missy. In fact, there's some cake in the fridge. Go have some with a glass of milk and try to call your father again."

"Can I give blood?" Hope asked from where she sat on a sofa before the TV where cartoons played with the volume at a whisper.

"No, honey," Jessie said, removing a pair of nitrile gloves. "I'm not even going to type you. Levon'll be here soon. That should be enough."

"I want to help," Hope insisted.

"Well, you can make sure your sister doesn't eat all the cake."

Hope left the sofa to follow Merry into the kitchen.

Jessie took a seat on the arm of a chair and regarded the dozing young man turning ashen in her late husband's La-Z-Boy.

"Who are you?" she said, mostly to the universe as the man named Wesley was sound asleep.

A spray of light played across the room. A car was in the gravel yard between the house and the stable building. It pulled around to come to a stop. Jessie ran to the front door and opened it to see her daughter Sandy climbing from a Kia Sorrento. Two other girls were getting out as well. One of them carried a pair of pizza boxes stacked in her arms.

"Sandy!" Jessie said, stepping off the porch onto the walk.

"Mom?" Sandy stopped on the gravel.

"You girls planning a night in?"

"Christy and Beth and I were going to watch a movie?" Sandy's voice rose in an uncertain lilt.

"Can you do it another night, baby? Girls? I have something going on here." She begged Sandy's understanding with pleading eyes.

"Sure, Mrs. Hamer," Christy said. "It's okay."

"And leave one of those pies," Jessie said.

The girls returned to the car but not before Sandy snaked one of the pizzas and followed Jessie back to the house.

"Is Levon here?" Sandy said with sly, accusatory eyes.

"It's not that," Jessie said and held the door for her.

"But it *is* Levon, right?"

"Yes," Jessie sighed. "It's Levon."

Merry met them at the door, eyes bright and chin smeared with frosting. She held up her phone.

"Daddy called!"

24

Fern piloted his Ford down the overgrown trail from the Scout camp.

"You'll owe me for a new paint job," Fern groused, wincing as branches along the trail scratched at the sides of the truck.

"I'm on the phone," Levon said and returned to his call.

"I need you to drive me over to Jessie's. Then head back to the farm and load up the animals and bring them to Jessie's," Levon said to Fern when the call ended.

"What's going on, nephew?"

Levon told his uncle about finding Wesley wounded and gave a brief need-to-know history of the man. Wesley needed blood and Levon was his type. He told Fern that there were men after him for something he did and something they wanted from him. And these men would not let up. They'd be back, in greater force. He needed to know the girls were safe. That meant they had to go to ground somewhere. Once they were all together at Jessie's there were dozens of places in the hills they could hide in for a while. Fern and the girls could rough it and leave Levon free to see to the men who would be stalking them.

"What did you do to these guys?"

"I was setting something right. I thought it was over."

"Mission accomplished," Fern said with a crooked smile.

"Yeah. Now I pissed off someone further up the chain of command and they can't let it rest."

"And how far does this chain go?"

"I wish to hell I knew, Fern."

"And the critters?" Fern said. "You sure you need me to haul them over there?"

"You know the girls. They'll sneak back for their horses if you don't."

"You got enough firepower and ammo?"

"There's plenty in the Avalanche for the job. I'll be fine."

Fern turned out of the brush onto the aggregate surface that would carry them back to the county road. He punched the gas with a spray of gravel. They raced through the dark down the tunnel of light cast by the Ford's headlights and roof rack array.

"I remember back when I was in country," Fern said, breaking the silence. "I asked for another mag for my 1911. The REMF at the depot, a lifer, some big Texan with bad teeth, says to me, 'Sonny, you get yourself into that kind of trouble, seven more rounds ain't gonna get your ass out of it.'"

"Yeah, I heard something like that a few times myself," Levon said.

"I say fuck that. Take enough to give every one of

those motherfuckers a triple tap," Fern said, sparing a glance from the wheel. "I need you to come home. Don't leave me with two broken-hearted little girls to raise, Levon."

25

The sun was down over the horizon leaving only a copper aura against the clouds that hovered over a burnished pewter sea.

Phil Barnes loved this time of the day. The harsh rays of the sun gone. A cooling breeze building off the water and carrying the smell of salt air over the sand. He sat on the deck that was at the end of a raised walkway that led back to his house, a three-bedroom building of stuccoed block with a tiled roof, lap pool, sauna and media room. A house that would cost him under a half mill back in his congressional district set him back three and a half million from his war chest here on the island. He raised a glass of pinot to the generous donors who'd made the contributions to his campaigns that made this lovely evening possible.

That was the beauty of running almost uncontested for his seat time and gain. Every two years he promoted the concept of a dark future in which his opponent won office and brought ruin to the state and district. He raised hundreds of thousands each

time and much of it vanished into thin air as he
needed little of the funds to actually secure his seat.
Most elections, his distinguished opposition ran a
half-hearted campaign in which they put up some
lightweight state senator or smalltown mayor. The
money he did spend was laundered through business
concerns owned by relatives who kicked much of
it back. One cousin placed ads on television and
radio for him for fifty percent cut of the ad price.
Most of that went into offshore accounts held by
the congressman.

All of that was spare change compared to the hard
cash that made its way to him from contractors,
lobbyists and anyone else who needed some support
on House votes, or a blind eye turned to some
malfeasance. Barnes was a master at ignoring lies,
corruption, inequities, and even downright felonies.

He'd bought this beach house on the western
shore of the island for the purpose of enjoying the
vista at dusk. And he had paid dearly as this was the
preferred end of the Caribbean sand spit. The biggest
marinas and resorts were on this shore. The land his
house was set on was registered as a conservation
area. Some cash spread around the council got him
a waiver.

It was all worth it for moments like this. Reclined
in a chair, looking over his stretch of private beach,
the white sugar sand, the soothing murmur of the
Gulf rolling in, an endless brow of phosphorescent
foam aglow in the dying light.

A voice called from behind him. He set his glass
down to turn his head back toward the house. Gina
stood on the walkway, silhouetted against the golden
glow from within the house.

"What is it, honey?" he called.

"One of your phones! It keeps buzzing!" the girl called back.

"You didn't answer it." It wasn't a question. It was a caution.

"You told me never to do that." Gina joined him on the deck.

"Good girl." He took the phone from her tiny hand. One of five burners that came along with him everywhere.

"Can I finish my movie?" she said, hand brushing the white hairs on his arm.

"Go on ahead," he said. "I have to make a call."

He watched her run back up to the house, bare feet slapping on the planks of the walkway. The last few strides, she broke into a skip that brought a smile to his lips. A smile that faded when he touched the screen on the phone.

"What is it?" he said when the call went through.

"Well, who woke up on the wrong side of the cabana?" Lew Dollinger's voice sounded tinny with a slight echo.

"Am I on speaker phone, you dumb fuck?" Barnes made no further attempt to hide his irritation.

"Relax, Congressman. I'm on the road, by myself. Picked up a fresh burner. Headed back down to Huntsville."

"You could have waited to report to me when I got back."

"Well, this won't keep, sir."

"What won't keep?"

"I don't want to go into any details right now other than to tell you that this afternoon was a goatfuck all the way."

"You failed?"

"Way more than failed. This fella you sicced me on is a real piece of work. It's lucky I'm here talking to you."

Lucky for who, Barnes thought but said, "Then you did not acquire what you promised me?"

"I came damn near acquiring wings and a harp." Dollinger's voice became hoarse for a moment, losing its usual air of snide jocularity.

The man was scared. For some reason, that made Barnes smile.

"That's unfortunate." Barnes's mind raced through his options.

"What you want me to do next?"

"Is there any way this man can identify you?"

"Could be. That's a possibility."

Dumb shitkicker, Barnes thought.

"Just go back to Huntsville and sit tight. Don't talk to anyone. In fact, hole up until you hear from me again. You understand?"

"Clear as mud, Congressman."

"You'll do just as I said. Go home. Stay home. I'll call you sometime tomorrow. In the afternoon, most likely."

"Will do."

The connection broke from Dollinger's end.

The congressman rose from the recliner with a grunted oath. He slammed the phone, screen down, onto the wooden railing that surrounded the deck. The case cracked and the glass screen shattered after three tries. He pitched it into the surf now swirling around the foot of the pilings that supported the deck. He flung his glass and what was left of the bottle of pinot after.

Sandals flapping on the walk, he returned to the house to make a call on another of his disposable phones.

It was going to be a very expensive call.

26

Merry ran from the house with Hope on her heels at the first sign of lights bouncing on the dark driveway.

She was surprised to see her father pull to a stop in the Mustang Merry helped him restore a few years back. The car's usual home was beneath a cover under the carport that stood by the barn, waxed and buffed to a mirror finish. She couldn't recall the last time her father had it out on the road.

"Your friend's looking bad," Merry said as Levon stepped from the car.

"I talked to Jessie. A transfusion and some rest and he'll be back on his feet." Levon swept Hope into his arms and maintained a grip on Merry's shoulder as they walked to the house.

"Why didn't Uncle Fern bring you right here?"

"He's trailering the horses over here."

"Why is that?" Hope said, raising her head from Levon's shoulder.

"Because we're gonna be going away," Merry said. Her voice was flat, without any sign of feeling other than dull resignation.

Hope's head tilted so she could look directly into Levon's face.

"We can talk about that later," Levon said as he moved past Merry holding the door with her eyes lowered to the floor of the porch.

***

"He's looking better," Jessie said, releasing Wesley's wrist to let it drop beside his sleeping form. "His color's better and pulse is regular."

"Thanks, Jessie." Levon rolled his sleeve down over the gauze about his arm where the trocar went in. The cloth had a pattern of orange and black cats on it. Wesley had a matching bandage on his arm that covered the infusion site as well as the continuing IV drip site.

"I owe you. Again," he said.

"What you owe me is an explanation," she said. "And none of your usual prevarication or bullshit."

"There's a difference?"

"You prevaricate when you avoid directly answering me." She dropped the used tubing and needles into a medical waste bin. Her eyes found his as she snapped off the nitrile gloves. "You bullshit when you outright lie to me. I'm not having either tonight."

Levon glanced through the guest room door. The girls were with Sandy watching something on the television in the family room. Music and laughter covered Merry and Hope's silence. He turned back to Jessie whose impatient gaze had not left him.

"I got myself into some trouble," he shrugged.

"Well, I didn't need to be sitting down to hear that," she said with a bitter smile. "But you do need to get off your feet and get some fluids in you."

She took him by the hand and led him into the kitchen where she cracked a pair of beers for them. He sipped the longneck while she took out cold cuts from the fridge. While she built sandwiches for them, he sat at the counter and leaned forward to speak to her.

Levon told her about the rabbit hole he'd entered after helping his cousin Teddy find answers about the disappearance of Trevor, Teddy's son. He left out the details of many of his actions over the past months to concentrate on the investigation he'd been involved in. Her face paled as he described how extensive the network of child trafficking he'd uncovered was. He explained that he'd managed to disrupt that network but didn't offer the methods he used to do so.

"You need to give what you have over to the police," Jessie said as she placed a plate before him with a pair of thick-sliced ham sandwiches topped with cheddar and a slather of mustard on it.

"There's a whole lot of reasons I can't do that," he said and took a bite of the first sandwich without tasting it.

"Levon," she said with a weary sigh, "you can't keep doing this."

"I know." He washed a mouthful of sandwich down with a swig of beer. "Only how am I supposed to look away?"

"You have your own children to think about. Your own life."

"Yeah. I know all that. I tell myself that. It's gone too far for that."

"What's that mean?"

"I pissed off some serious folks this time. They're going to be coming for me."

"The girls can stay here as long as you need. Your friend, too, until this is over."

"That's just it, Jessie." He reached over the counter to take her hand, and the gesture surprised her. "I'm not sure this'll ever be over."

"What's that mean?" She did not return his grip on her hand.

He released her hand to take another slug of beer.

"Fern's coming by with the trailer. If it's all right with you, I need to board the horses here a while. I'll leave you money for looking after them. Fern'll come get them after a while."

"You're leaving," she said.

"For a while anyway. It's best you don't know where."

"*You* don't know where, do you? And you don't know for how long."

"I'm sorry, Jessie."

"That's all I'm hearing tonight."

"I don't know what else to do."

"Then finish your goddamn sandwich," she said, and turning from him, left the room.

27

He knew he'd have to catch the goat first.

The black and white Abyssinian he'd re-named Tricky Dick would make loading the two horses and pony a bigger pain in his ass than it already was.

Fern had clean forgotten the name the girls had originally given to the contrary horned motherfucker. The goat earned his new sobriquet for his surprise attacks on anyone unfortunate to bend over within his sight. Merry and Hope thought it was Dick's playful nature. Fern knew it was a meanness at the heart of the beast, a malevolence that was plainly visible in its weird marble blue eyes.

Even now it had climbed atop a tall stack of hay bales inside the stable. It stood spraddle-legged, the little bell on its collar tinkling as it lowered its head his way. He tried to tempt it down with some sweet feed and carrots. The goat was not taking the bait. It stood above him, studying Fern with deep suspicion.

"Come on down here you, you stubborn sumbitch," Fern said sweetly, coaxing the animal with the bunch of limp carrots in one hand and metal scoop of molasses-sticky oats in the other.

He knew he'd have to get Dick secured in the cab of his pickup even if the goat shit over all the upholstery. It was the only way as otherwise the goat would prance around, getting the horses worked up as he tried to load them on the trailer. Especially Bravo, the big black Levon bought for himself upon Merry's urging. That horse hated the trailer, and it was going to be a bitch getting it up the ramp even without the little cloven-hooved menace bleating and kicking all over the yard. Tricky Dick was a social animal who tolerated change poorly. Any sign that the horses were being carted off would send the goat into a frenzy.

As it was, the battle of wits between Fern and Dick was working on the horses' nerves. They were snuffling and blowing in their stalls as they picked up on the contention between man and animal playing out in the main aisle.

It was for that very reason Fern had the dogs, the bluetick and the Jack Russell locked up in the house. The last thing he needed was the two dogs getting into the mix and frazzling the big dumb horses' nerves any further.

"You come down and have some yummy carrots," Fern wheedled. "Or I'll get a gun and shoot you offa there."

He'd do no such thing. The girls loved the goat and found its mercurial nature and psychotic personality amusing. It was fun to fantasize putting a round between those horns though. He'd need to get a grip on the tricky bastard without resorting to lethal means. Only the sweet feed and carrots were not enticement enough.

Fern recalled the one treat that Dick was powerless to resist. He backed to the stable door with the goat watching his every step. Outside in the moonlight, Fern crossed to the house and entered the kitchen. Rascal, the Jack Russell leapt at him, jaws slavering. Bella, the bluetick hound, lay curled in her dog bed beating a lazy rhythm on the tiles with her tail. It was well past her bedtime.

Leaving the lights off, he searched the cabinets with no luck until he remembered that Merry kept a big old jar of Skippy at the back of the refrigerator. She preferred it chilled. He found the half-full jar behind the milk and retrieved a mixing spoon from a cabinet drawer.

A bare bulb lit up by the back door, throwing the kitchen into a red glow. It was connected to a pressure line that ran across the end of the drive down near the road.

He stood peering through the screen door and heard the crunch of gravel out on the long driveway. Someone was approaching the house, moving slow. They were keeping their headlights off.

Fern thought about what Levon had told him. This could be the same guys from Sugar Run come to take up their unfinished business with Levon.

He reached a hand up to where a Remington pump rested in hooks over the doorway. He worked the pump back enough to expose the shiny brass end of a round of bird shot already home in the chamber. Fern always loaded a bird round to come out first. He called it his second chance round just in case of accidents or mistaken identity. Better to pepper someone with an assload of BBs than blow their head off with a buck round or a slug. That way you'd only need to apologize rather than mourn. Most times, in his experience, the boom of a shotgun was enough to run off trespassers. A turkey load was near as loud as a more lethal shell for that.

Bella rose with a whimper from her bed. Rascal totted toward the door, a low growl building in his throat. Fern hushed them both. While not entirely silent, neither dog took up barking. They were satisfied with low rumbles in their chests and the occasional canine version of a harumph.

Fern snapped off the wall switch that worked the lamp set atop a utility pole at one of the stable yards. It had a motion feature attached to it and he preferred keeping things dark for his unexpected visitors until he could determine the reason for their visit. Stepping back into the dimness of the kitchen, Fern had a clear view of the SUV pulling to a stop just behind the pickup backed to the stable, the horse trailer already hitched with the ramp dropped.

Two men climbed out of the SUV. A dark Chevy with fat wheels. The driver stood with a long gun of some kind in the crook of his arm. The passenger made his way around the back of the vehicle where the tailgate door was already swinging up to expose the cargo bed. The man at the back lifted out a pair of heavy cans. Gas cans. The passenger handed one of the cans to the driver. From the weight of them in their hands they appeared to be full.

There were some words exchanged between the two as they walked toward the stable building. Fern couldn't make out the conversation over the wind through the swish of the trees and the insistent bleating of the goat inside the barn wondering what happened to its playmate.

Fern thumbed back the safety on the Remmy and shouldered the screen door open as slow as he could to not let the springs jangle. He let it close behind him just as slowly, a foot held back to keep the terrier from following from the house.

The men were out of sight in the deep shadows on the far side of the horse trailer. He could hear muttered voices. A sharp stink reached his nose.

Gasoline.

Fern stepped around the back of the trailer. The two men had the cans open and were splashing gas onto the wood of the double doors at the front of the stable.

"Put 'em down," Fern said, the shotgun held to his shoulder and trained on the pair of men.

One of them tossed his can Fern's way, making Fern step to one side to avoid being struck. The other dropped his can to the ground where it glugged its contents onto the gravel. This man was moving for the rifle leaning against the rear wall of the trailer.

The first man, the gas can flinger, clawed at his waistband beneath his open coat.

Fern wasn't taking chances on what the man might have there and fired the shotgun. A game load took the man full in the face and he dropped wailing to his knees. That was the warning shot spent.

The second man got a load of buck that threw him backwards onto the trailer ramp. The rifle, some variation of an AK, clattered to the ground.

Blood mixed with tears streamed from the first man's face as he played his hands blindly across the gravel looking for the revolver that had dropped from under his belt when the BBs took him.

His hand found the butt of the .38 just before a

second load of buckshot took him center mass. He flipped onto his back with a keening animal cry. The second man lay motionless on the trailer, flat on his back, arms wide and the smell from his emptied bowels mixing with the tang of fresh blood in the air.

The training of thirty-six months spent in the Republic of Vietnam kicked in and Fern gave the man lying on the trailer ramp a second round. A pumpkin ball this time. The force of the fat ball of lead shifted the man's dead form bodily on the blood-slick ramp.

Fern stood over the other man who was gasping out his life in the spreading pool of gasoline that had spilled from the pair of dropped cans. The man's face was a bloody ruin from the turkey load. His breath bubbled crimson from his shredded lips and nostrils. Fern could see the wet gleam of bone through the mess the buck had made of the man's chest.

He waited until the man's legs stopped their feeble dance. The chest collapsed with one long final sigh.

Using the trailer, then the truck, for cover, Fern moved, shotgun trained, to the SUV. He satisfied himself that these two were the only occupants. He looked down the driveway toward the trees along the road. All was dark and nighttime quiet. These two had come alone. He returned to where the dead men lay.

Turning over the one with the birdshot face, Fern found the man's wallet, a snakeskin model fat with bills. Clouds crossed in front of the moon. He couldn't read the driver's license in the new gloom. He stepped to the house, the dogs going mad inside. The gunfire set them off. The stench of blood and unleaded only stirred them up more as he stepped into the kitchen and flipped on the lights to learn the name of the man he'd just watched die.

The face of Deacon Taggart smirked back at him in the cold light of the ceiling fluorescents.

28

Traffic was light on the highway heading south. Mostly semis staying to the right. A light rain was coming down, and Levon had to keep the wipers on high as each tractor trailer he passed sent up a fresh spray of filthy slush. Rush hour had come to an end by the time he reached the Huntsville exits.

Levon followed the directions he recalled as given by the second man he killed back in Sugar Run. Third exit along and follow a county road into a community of mixed single homes and apartments. From there he found the grandly named Beaufort Farms, a self-described complex of "garden apartments" according to the sign at the main entrance. There was a gate, but it lay open. The guard shack was empty. There were no surveillance cameras that he could see.

He saw nothing "garden" about the faceless, stucco saltboxes fronted with parking lots that lined the curved roads inside the development. There were some median strips crowded with weeds gone brown in the winter cold and a few open areas between buildings covered in crabgrass dotted with drooping pines.

The collection of identical structures was larger than he anticipated. Each building had a grandiose name like Windmere or Buckingham or Driftwood. The fading numbers painted on the sides of each building were impossible to read in the dark. He'd only find where this Lew Dollinger lived by driving by every place and checking the name over the bank of mailboxes that sat across from each one.

At the end of a cul-de-sac, he found the apartment building named Hampshire. He cut the lights on the Avalanche and pulled around the rear of the building. The jacked-up truck, the same one that nearly plowed into him back at Sugar Run, sat parked in a spot next to an overflowing dumpster. There were fresh holes in the rear quarter panel. Jagged rents in the metal from shrapnel. A vintage Caddy in sky blue was parked a few spaces from the truck.

Dollinger's apartment was on the ground floor with access along a hallway shared with other units. Main doors at the front and rear of the building required a key for entry. There were sliders at the rear of each unit that opened onto a balcony on the higher floors and a patio with a curtain wall for the ground floor apartments. No cameras in sight. No reason to think the main entry doors were alarmed. This was an older building, 1980s or older.

He could try to gain entry by pressing the buttons at the intercom. Chances were too great he'd run into one of the other occupants that way. It might be better to wait until later. He could try the sliders but had no way of knowing which led to Dollinger's unit. He realized that he didn't know what Dollinger looked like beyond Wesley's description of him as "the whitest motherfucker" he'd ever seen.

He backed the Avalanche into an empty spot in a row that ran along the side of the building. From there he had a view of the back of the Hampshire and the knobby-tired truck. If Dollinger returned to the truck he'd have him. In the meantime, he'd work out how to get into the building. Closer to midnight or after. For now, he'd watch the lot.

Hours passed and televisions in some of the units cast blue shadows on the windows. More units went dark. There was still light coming from two of the ground floor apartments. He'd wait a while until those went out and move on the entry door.

A dark car, an SUV with heavily tinted windows pulled around the far end of the building and came to stop at the end of the walk that led to the entry door. It sat there, blue exhaust drifting from the tailpipe and lights out. Rainwater beaded on its beetle-black hood and rooftop.

Everything about it was wrong.

Keeping his eyes on the SUV, a long Suburban, Levon reached through the gap between the front seats to draw his M4 to him. He pulled back on the action to chamber round one and tabbed the selection lever to semi-auto. His gaze never left the idling vehicle parked fifty yards away.

Shadows grew from behind the hedges that lined the walk to climb the wall of the building. Three men came into view as they exited the apartments. Two men bracing a third between them. The man in the middle doing a skipping frog-walk, walking on tiptoes in his stocking feet. Bare legs were visible. The man in the middle wore only boxers and a T-shirt in addition to his black socks. In the halogen glare of a lamp high on the back wall of the building, the skin of the man's bare arms and legs shone almost silver against the dark clothing of the men escorting him to the SUV. Blood stains on his white T looked black in the harsh light.

The man in boxers was tall and rangy, broad shouldered and a slight paunch above skinny bird legs. He was not cuffed; his hands were free. The men walking with him wore no insignia, no badges in evidence. No one spoke.

Levon stepped from the Avalanche into the misting rain. He had the M4 raised to his shoulder and put three rounds into the driver's side of the windshield of the Suburban as he walked.

The horn let out a long mournful blare as the SUV drifted slowly forward under its own power. The two clothed men reacted with counterproductive intentions. One of them released the man in boxers to claw at the driver side door of the SUV as it rolled away. The other tightened his grip on his charge while drawing a black automatic from under his coat.

Two rounds to the head dropped the one with the automatic. The lifeless man crumpled to the ground, releasing the man in boxers. The other was trotting alongside the Suburban, the door open, now. He moved in a stumbling gait, trying to stay on his feet while he took the steering wheel from the dead driver's hands.

The man in the T-shirt and boxers took off running at the first opportunity. As fast as his scrawny legs could carry him, he vanished into the gloom at the far end of the building.

The Suburban had trundled at an angle against

the curtain wall that ran behind the ground-floor units. The would-be substitute driver had to give up as it came to a grinding halt, the driver's door pressed shut against the wall. The second man, using the car for cover, backed away, drawing a handgun from his clothing as he did so.

Levon shot out the glass of the idling SUV to force the man to keep his head down. It gave Levon time to move closer at an angle that revealed the rear of the Suburban to him.

The man was moving hunched along the curtain wall back toward the rear entrance of the building. Levon dropped him with a triple-tap to center mass. The man sagged against the wall, legs kicking at gravel. Two more to the head and the man was still.

Lights were coming on along the back of the building. Levon ran back to the Avalanche and climbed inside. He took off in the direction the nearly naked man had run.

Levon caught him in the brilliance of his high beams, white legs and arms pumping. The man who had to be Lew Dollinger ran between two rows of parked cars. He lost a sodden sock as he shifted course to run between two cars.

Slamming the brakes and jerking the wheel hard, Levon spun the front of the truck to find the running man once again in his headlights. Dollinger, aglow in the twin beams, ran under some pines into one of the open areas.

Levon gunned his truck through an empty space between two parked cars and hopped the curb to tear through the trees. On the way he sideswiped a parked Lexus hard enough to set its car alarm whooping.

He found Dollinger again, running a crooked path across the grassy lot. He pressed the accelerator to the floor and jerked the wheel to shift the direction of the truck. A shoulder driven into his door popped it open in time catch the running man full in the back. Dollinger tumbled to the ground in a flurry of pale limbs.

Levon brought the Avalanche to a juddering stop and leapt out to drag the stunned man across the grass. Dollinger was weeping and gasping from either pain, fear, exertion or all three. Levon bundled the man into the rear bed of the truck and slammed the tailgate closed behind him. He heard feeble pleas for mercy through the tonneau cover as he swung himself back into the cab and punched the truck into motion.

29

Lew Dollinger kicked his bare feet against the roof of the hard tonneau cover.

He let off after a while, lying on his side in the dark, feeling every bump in the road beneath him. The pain in his back was spreading into his groin. The sumbitch hit him with a truck. The door of a truck anyway.

He was angry and he was scared. Mostly he was angry. That pig-fucker Phil Barnes set his dogs on him. Assholes showed up at his door and dragged him off in his skivvies to a shallow grave somewhere. Real hardcases who rousted him with practiced ease. These guys were fixers way up in the pecking order of door-kickers and hard chargers. Ex-cops or ex-feds gone over to the dark side for a fat wad of dark money. They trotted him out of Hampshire #103 slick as snot and easy as you please without a word spoken between them.

Then some other asshole pops up out of nowhere to ruin their day. Lewis Dollinger didn't just fall off the turnip truck. He knew this new arrival meant him just as much trouble as the first bunch. He had no idea where he was going when he ran off. He only knew he wanted away from anyone more badass than the hard-ons who sandbagged him.

It was all Barnes's fault. All of it. That smooth-talking prick dropped him into this mess and treated him like a mushroom. Kept him in the dark and fed him nothing but shit. Not a word about niggers with dynamite or secret Klan hideouts or some hillbilly hardass with special hate for baby-rapers. He was just turned loose, without a clue or the full story, in the hopes he might just stumble over whatever goodies the congressman was looking for. And when he fucks up once, just one time, Barnes sends some kind of magicians to disappear his ass off the planet forever and ever.

The truck slowed to a stop. Hiss and boom of passing traffic. They were stopped at a light. He started kicking again and howling for help. He gave up when the fire in his back built to a searing blaze that climbed up his neck. He lay splayed on his back on the rumbling bed panting while he searched his mind for options.

This guy took him alive for a reason. There was something more he wanted. All Dollinger had to do was play him along, build a rapport. There had to be a deal, one that would let him walk away with a whole skin. His set-up here was over so the shelf life on any old loyalties was way past sell-by. He'd burn his bridges and sink his boats and give it all up to the guy driving this truck in exchange for a pass.

Lew Dollinger had never heard of Stockholm Syndrome. But he'd surrendered his flabby white ass to it now.

The truck bucked and yawed as it moved over rougher ground. They were off road now. He could still hear the rush of traffic from somewhere. They came to a stop with a jerk that sent Dollinger crashing against a side panel. The cab door creaked and slammed. The tailgate dropped with a bang to let in gray light.

"Get out. Feet first," a voice said from the outside.

"Gimme a minute here, boss," Dollinger said, sliding on his butt over the pebbled bed cover. "You juked my back real good, alright?"

"Hands out," the man said as Dollinger emerged from under the tonneau to sit on the tailgate, bare legs dangling.

"No trouble here, boss."

Dollinger looked up from under his brows to see the man standing in silhouette against the pearly gloaming of moonlight coming through the overcast sky. He held a handgun at ease at his side.

They'd come to some kind of road construction site. A big grader and a crane sat at the edge of a field of bare dirt. Rows of Jersey barriers sat off to one side of the cleared area. Behind him trucks and cars, invisible from this angle, moved along a raised section of highway.

"Stand up and take two steps toward me," the man said.

"Awful cold, boss. I got no shoes. No clothes neither."

"Then you'll want this over sooner."

"Okay. All right." Dollinger took two mincing steps forward, his toes already going numb on the freezing wet ground.

"Do you know who I am?"

Dollinger had taken note of the truck. An Avalanche. The same truck he'd followed a few nights back. The same truck that nearly t-boned him this afternoon.

"You're Levon Cade." No sense playing at lying. Time for that later. Start with the truth and build your lies on that.

"Who sent you after me?"

"We can get to that later," Dollinger said, trying out a smile.

"Walk over this way." The man used the automatic in his hand to point off toward the shadows cast by the overpass.

"Might take a minute. You maybe busted my back, boss." His feet were numb now, pins and needles running up his calves.

Dollinger hobbled ahead until he came to the lip of a drop off. Down in the dark he could hear the gurgling passage of a creek through reeds rimed with new ice from the drizzling rain. They looked like glass, shimmering in the indirect light cast by the cars and trucks moving by above.

"Do you understand what we're doing here?" the man said from behind him.

"Yeah. Yes, boss." Dollinger's voice rasped. A shiver spread across his body. He wanted to blame the cold.

"Who sent you after me?"

"What'll you do if I tell you?"

"Think about what I'll if you don't."

There was no percentage in pissing this guy off, Dollinger thought. And the odds of two unexpected rescues in one night was too much to hope for.

"His name's Phil Barnes."

"Who's that?"

"Congressman. Tenth district."

"What does he want with me?"

"Lawyer friend of his had some papers and shit

that Barnes wants back real bad."

"Shit like videos?"

"I don't know what all." Dollinger was shivering now, biting down to keep his jaw still. "I'm just an errand boy."

"You ever see one of the videos? Ever see what's on them?"

"I swear to Jesus I never seen 'em. Never heard of 'em till now. I got no idea what Barnes wanted 'em for or what they're about."

The man was silent awhile.

Dollinger's knees surrendered to the agony climbing up from his feet and down from his bruised spine. He dropped to his knees on the icy blades of dead grass.

"You gotta believe me, boss. All's I was sent to do was to get them papers. I never meant you or your nigger no harm. I swear to God above and on my mama's eyes, I was only doin' as I was told, and I wasn't told shit!"

His shoulders hunched and he let out a high-pitched yelp at a sudden bang behind him. Turning on all fours he watched the Avalanche pull across the construction lot for the surface road that lay beyond the open gate in a high cyclone fence.

Lew Dollinger began crying then, tears that turned to ice on his pale skin. He doubled over, forehead on the cold ground, his body wracked with sobs. Sobs that turned to a sucking, choking growl that built to a hearty guffaw as he struggled shaking to his feet.

That dumb cracker was off to kill himself a sitting United States congressman and Dollinger hoped he succeeded.

30

Fern was awaiting outside Jessie's barn when Levon pulled up. It was well toward morning with the sky turning gray over the line of razorback ridges that ran behind the property.

"You just getting here?" Levon said.

"The horses is put up," Fern said. "They're watered and fed and in their stalls. You know you got a bad dent in your driver door?"

"The girls help you?"

"Naw. They're asleep in the house. I didn't see any cause to wake them."

"What took you so long?"

"That's kind of a long story," Fern said, eyes lowered and kicking at the gravel with the toe of one boot.

"Well, tell it walking. I want to check on Wesley."

"Who? That the fella needed your blood?" Fern said, following Levon toward the darkened house.

"Keep quiet. I don't want to wake anyone," Levon said and held the door open for his uncle.

***

"I thought it was the same bunch came for you at Sugar Run," Fern said, voice low. He was leaning back on a dresser in Jessie's guest room.

"Bad night for Deacon and his asshole buddy to show up." Levon was checking the pulse of the man who lay sound asleep in the cannonball bed. An IV line ran into an arm that lay atop the covers.

"He's Army," Fern sniffed, nodding at the eagle tattoo on the sleeping man's arm.

"He can't help that."

"You know, maybe we shouldn't be talkin' about this in front of someone who ain't family."

"Wes is as deep in this as any of us. He took a load of buck meant for me. Besides, he's still riding on a double dose of the good stuff."

"I know you're in the shit up to your eyeballs," Fern said. "And here I go throwing on another shovel load."

"You got Deacon and his friend out of sight?"

"Dragged 'em to the manure heap and pulled some down on them. We'll need to go back and do a better job burying them. Drove their SUV back into the trees the other side of the paddock."

"We'll need to drop that somewhere else." Levon took a seat in a ladderback chair that sat by the bed. "We got a lot of digging ahead of us."

"Let me head back and bury those two chumps good."

"Not just burying. Digging up too. And loading the trucks."

"That bad, huh?"

"About as bad as it gets, Fernie. What all I stirred up and now the Taggarts. We're gonna have shit flying at us from every direction."

"We need to get out of the county a while," Fern said.

"We need to get out of the state. Far as we can go." Levon looked up at Fern, the gaze far away as he planned their next move.

"You mean *di di mau*. Bugout. Never coming back."

Levon lowered his eyes, nodding.

"I don't envy you telling the girls."

"And Jessie," Levon said, lifting his eyes to look at the closed door of the guest room.

"Merry's been on the dodge with you before."

"Except this time, I told her we were home for good. And Hope's having less nightmares now. She's finally feeling settled."

"Couldn't be helped, Levon."

"The hell it couldn't. I brought this on us. I put the girls at risk playing hero."

"You were doin' what's right. Your girls understand that. Hell, Merry didn't find Hopey in a Crackerjack box."

Levon snorted.

"That's right," Fern said with a hiss. "Your little Merry took that child away from a cartel. And she's done more than that and you know it."

Levon looked up, eyes narrowing as he nodded. There was at least one body buried back up the holler that his daughter put there.

"What kinda timeline we lookin' at to get shed of here?" Fern asked.

"Yesterday wouldn't be soon enough for me. We pack up only what we need or can't live without."

"And your friend here?" Fern canted his head toward Wesley.

"I'll leave him with enough cash he can decide what he wants to do once he's healed up."

"Fuck that," Wesley said. Only it came out more like "fuh dat" through the morphine haze.

"What did you hear?" Levon said, turning to him.

"Enough to know you're gonna need another driver," Wesley said before dropping back into the warm embrace of sleep.

31

"That's quite a tan, congressman," his assistant said, looking up from her desk and over the correspondence piled before her.

"Thank you, Kay." He looked at the sagging stack of letters and parcels with a weary sigh. "Anything urgent there?"

"You know they *all* think they're urgent. But these came by messenger. They look official." She handed him three thick envelopes. Two Fed Ex, and a DHL. "And you have email too."

"Well, that's my morning shot to hell." He offered her a wink and a lazy smile before stepping toward his office.

"And the phone was ringing when I came in this morning. I just let it go to voicemail."

"Listen to them for me, Kay. Half of 'em'll want to know how my golf game went. The rest'll be asking for favors or quotes. And take down any numbers I need to have. You know who's priority."

"You gonna want coffee, sir?"

"Had some on the drive in. I'll buzz you if I need

more." He shut the door behind him. The phone was ringing as he did so.

After taking the phone off the hook, he dropped into the leather chair behind his desk and took off his brogans to put on the carpet slippers he always wore on days when he expected no visitors. He tore open the only one of the three envelopes he had any interest in. The results of a survey of some land he was eyeing down in Florida.

Thanks to his office and favors owed, he had advance knowledge of an upcoming expansion to a large retirement community in Hernando County on the Gulf. Per acre land values in the surrounding area would skyrocket when the plans became public. He considered picking up a few parcels through a holding company in his wife's name. Once the developer announced the plans for the expansion, Barnes could sell the lots off for seven or eight times what he paid for them.

The other packages were the usual entreaties for help with this and that. Cancer research. Veterans. A woman's clinic in Birmingham. Everyone had their hand out.

It came to Phil Barnes's realization, after half a life spent in office, that his time was divided between some people begging him for help or him begging other people for money. Being a congressman meant serving a two-year term. What it really meant was a perpetual campaign for office. Endless fundraisers, press junkets and chicken dinners. Though a wealthy man in reality if not on paper, the congressman never spent his own money on a campaign. He took cash out but never put cash in. The first rule of politics as far as he was concerned.

He touched the mouse to bring his screen to life. Kay was right. The email from over his long weekend had piled up. He scrolled down page after page to delete or highlight each. Mostly delete. Messages from his constituents. Invites to dinners and events where he'd be expected to speak.

Commencements, the opening of a new car wash in Twickenham, a luncheon for the Daughters of the Confederacy and a ceremony for a new county highway project breaking ground. He'd need to speak to Kay about getting someone in to adjust his spam filters.

An email from a sender he didn't recognize made him delay hitting delete. The subject line sent an electric thrill through his body.

The Hacienda

The return address was a Day's Inn from Thompson's Station up in Tennessee. Someone sent it from their registration desk.

His address, phbarnes@hr.house.gov, was only one in a long list that included the *Huntsville Herald*, *The Birmingham Times*, *USA Today*, *The Washington Times*, the local Fox affiliate, *The Rolling Stone*, *The Daily Mail*, Alabama State CID as well as a few dozen other state agencies, television stations, news websites, newspapers and other members of congress as well as the governor's office. Even the bitch running to oppose him in the fall was CC'd.

There was no message in the body of the mail. Only an attachment. A video.

He could hear the phone ringing in the outer office as he left-clicked the attachment to open it.

The video began without preamble in a window on his screen.

He heard his own voice before the image came into focus.

"You like to dance, don't you?"

On the screen he could see a moving shadow on a wall of knotty pine paneling. A figure moved from the extreme foreground, twirling. Narrow hips moving under a pair of denim cut-offs. Tiny fists gathering the hem of an oversized T-shirt and pulling the shirt up to reveal a pair of bee sting breasts. The girl gyrated awkwardly to a dance beat coming from off screen. She raised her head to look into the camera, a loose smile on her lips. Unfocused eyes looked out from under feathery blonde bangs. They were ringed by thick bands of mascara that accented pale skin beneath a spray of freckles.

The honorable Phillip Barnes did not recall the girl. The room she danced in he could never forget.

"You gonna dance for me, are you?" he heard himself say.

The camera angle moved abruptly before coming to rest at a different angle that took in a wicker daybed resting against a curtained wall. He watched himself move into camera range and take a seat on the edge of the daybed. A younger version of himself. Maybe ten years ago. His hair was thicker, and he was still dying it then.

"Why'nt you dance a little closer?" he said.

The girl came into the picture then, shuffling nearer, narrow arms raised over her head. He saw himself clutch at the T-shirt swaying before him. Then they were on the daybed together.

Barnes glanced again at the list of addresses the email had been sent to. The phone was ringing in the outer office. He realized that it had never stopped ringing. It would never stop ringing. He looked to the right-hand drawer of his desk and reached for the brass pull handle.

In the outer office, Kay was taking down numbers from that morning's voicemails as well as fielding fresh calls as they came in. From the nature of the questions asked on the calls, she was thinking about where she'd be working this time next week. And wondering if she'd need a lawyer.

She heard a loud but muffled pop from within her boss's office followed by something that sounded like a hound when its tail gets stomped on.

32

**STATE MOURNS CONGRESSMAN,
10th DISTRICT DEAD FROM
HEART ATTACK**
Huntsville Herald (Evening Edition)

Long-serving house representative
Phillip Maddox Barnes (R, AL)
passed away this morning from what
county medical examiners are calling
a massive coronary event. He was
declared dead on arrival at Crestwood
Medical Center after failing to be
revived by EMTs. "We have lost a
hard-working servant of the people
and a true warrior for democracy
today," said the state governor in a
statement that expressed sentiments
shared by Alabamians everywhere.
Congressman Barnes will be most
remembered for his work with local
veterans' organizations as well as
his support for city and state youth
programs.

33

An hour over the state border, Kansas just looked like more Missouri to Fern. Levon was in the Mustang twenty car lengths ahead, his right turn signal on for the next exit off 84. Fern followed after a glance in his side view. The lights of the Avalanche were visible in the distance past the horse trailer Fern was pulling. He signaled right and Wesley responded with his own blinkers.

"Sign said there's a Wendy's up ahead," Fern said. He turned down Steve Earle on the radio.

"I'm not real hungry," Merry said from the back seat, meeting his gaze in the rearview. Both girls were in the back seat with the bluetick hound curled between them. Rascal rode shotgun in the passenger seat, snorting as he dozed.

"You'll change your mind when we get there."

She responded with a grunt.

"Hope asleep?" Though he already knew she was as he hadn't heard her crying since they passed Blue Springs. Merry's eyelids were red too, though she'd never admit it.

"Uh huh."

"Maybe when we stop you want to switch. Ride with your daddy."

"We'll stay with you, Uncle Fern."

"Why's that? You like my choice of music?"

"Daddy doesn't want us with him in case there's a problem. He'll want to draw trouble away from us."

"He tell you that?"

"He didn't have to," Merry said.

Damn, Fern thought to himself, the shit these girls have seen. Merry on the run with her father for years before coming home. He knew some of what they went through up in Maine and across five or six other states. Levon and Merry told him enough separately to know it was rough and not much else. Little Hopey's childhood wasn't lollipops and rainbows either. Sold to coyotes who brought her up from Guatemala and across Mexico to drag her around shopping malls to shoplift for them. All that was behind them until Levon stirred up this mess. And Fern didn't help much by killing Deke Taggart and whoever that other shit-bird was. Now they were a sad goddamn convoy driving through the night leaving everything they knew behind.

He and Levon spent the previous day packing the vehicles and trailer and digging up coffee cans and airtight drums from spots all over the farm. Levon had recorded the GPS locations of the caches of containers that held bundles of cash, flash drives and other goods sealed in plastic bags. Fern caught a glimpse of an envelope filled with what looked like uncut diamonds. They spilled onto the kitchen table when Levon was repacking the swag. Two Yeti coolers packed with currency. One into the trunk of the Mustang and the other in the back seat of the Avalanche. A measure of the level of trust Levon had in the man he'd only met a few months back. They, each of them, the three men and the girls, had more than ten grand in bills hidden on their persons in case they had to split up and make their own way.

"Could it be you're maybe a little angry with your daddy?" Fern said as he pulled down a long exit ramp for a surface road that ran under the highway.

"Not angry at anyone," she said with a catch in her voice. "Just angry, I guess."

"You'll get new horses wherever we wind up." Fern shot a look at the mirror, but Merry's face was in shadow.

"Won't be the same. Won't be our horses."

That hurt. Fern felt a twinge in his throat. Though he for shit-sure wouldn't miss that damn goat, he felt for the girls. They lived for those animals. Knowing they'd be under permanent care at Jessie Hamer's farm wouldn't do much to ease that hurt. Only time could accomplish that.

He pulled off the surface road and onto the Wendy's lot. Levon was already a car ahead of them at the drive-through. There was a county sheriff's car parked on the lot. They didn't dare risk going inside let alone be seen together. Fern rolled up behind the mini-van idling behind the Mustang and came to a stop.

"I know you said you ain't hungry, I'm gonna order some for you and Hope anyway." Fern rolled the window down.

Silence from the back seat.

"You hear me, Merry?"

"Where do you think we're going?" she said, her

voice small.

"I don't know, honey."

"He must have told you something."

"All's I know is west," Fern said, pretending to read the brightly colored menu through misting eyes. "He said 'west.'"

TAKE A LOOK AT BOOK ELEVEN: LEVON'S RANGE

Chuck Dixon delivers the eleventh book in his dark and suspense-filled series—Levon Cade.

Levon Cade and his daughters are on the run and living under assumed names in a remote corner of Idaho where Levon has taken on the role of gentlemen rancher. But when someone rustles his girls' favorite horses, Levon puts aside his gentlemanly ways in exchange for hunting them down.

Too bad Lew Dollinger, a man Levon unwisely allowed to live, is—at the same time—tasked with locating the runaway Cades by an international crime cartel.

As the past closes in on Levon, he'll have to decide if he's run out of places to hide.

AVAILABLE AUGUST 2022

ABOUT THE AUTHOR

Born and raised in Philadelphia, Chuck Dixon worked a variety of jobs from driving an ice cream truck to working graveyard at a 7-11 before trying his hand as a writer. After a brief sojourn in children's books he turned to his childhood love of comic books. In his thirty years as a writer for Marvel, DC Comics and other publishers, Chuck built a reputation as a prolific and versatile freelancer working on a wide variety titles and genres from Conan the Barbarian to SpongeBob SquarePants. His graphic novel adaptation of J.R.R. Tolkien's The Hobbit continues to be an international bestseller translated into fifty languages. He is the co-creator (with Graham Nolan) of the Batman villain Bane, the first enduring member added to the Dark Knight's rogue's gallery in forty years. He was also one of the seminal writers responsible for the continuing popularity of Marvel Comics' The Punisher.

After making his name in comics, Chuck moved to prose in 2011 and has since written over twenty novels, mostly in the action-thriller genre with a few side-trips to horror, hardboiled noir and western. The transition from the comics form to prose has been a life-altering event for him. As Chuck says, "writing a comic is like getting on a roller coaster while writing a novel is more like a long car trip with a bunch of people you'll learn to hate." His Levon Cade novels are currently in production as a television series from Sylvester Stallone's Balboa Productions. He currently lives in central Florida and, no, he does not miss the snow.

Printed in Great Britain
by Amazon

20185777R00103